S0-ACP-693

Khayal

By
Cristel Orrand

Cristel Orrand

*Amalgamist
Books*

Edited by Lauren Lowther

Proofread by Melinda Elingburg

signature

Dedication

To dreamers and redeemers-
No soul or cause is ever lost.

To the chosen families-
Love needs no blood.

To my own Jaddah and Jiddo-
Who taught me both.

&

To Sunshine and Moonbeam-
You are my light.

Contents

Khayal

By
Cristel Orrand

All rights reserved. No part of this book may be reproduced, scanned, or distributed in any printed or electronic form without permission. Please do not participate in or encourage piracy of copyrighted materials in violation of the author's rights. Purchase only authorized editions.

This is a work of fiction. Names, characters, places, and incidents either are the product of the author's imagination or are used fictitiously, and any resemblance to actual persons, living or dead, businesses, companies, events or locales is coincidental.

Although every precaution has been taken to verify the accuracy of the information contained herein, the author and publisher assume no responsibility for any errors or omissions. No liability is assumed for damages that may result from the use of information contained within.

A Recipe for a Novel (Author's Note):

It all started with a question: is the chemical composition of ruby ash any different from any other kind of ash? Yes, in case you were wondering, it is; but this isn't Sci-Fi, and as I am inordinately susceptible to falling down rabbit holes, I went with it.

In the boroughs of the underworld, I wrestled with ghosts, philosophers and nameless things. On the way up, I added things I love, such as olives, rocks, rugs and 4-speed manual transmissions. I waited and listened when grandfather spoke. And when I had faith, I gave it a name.

The best thing about writing a book is that you can do anything you want, put any music on in the car, find homes for lost thoughts, or let them go in peace. *Ma'assalama.*

Wadi Rum

In the moonlit valley,
She unzipped her taut skin,
And into the black night
Shed the shadows within.

Caves cradled desert winds,
Sandblasted the ruddy stones
Moored Bedouin fires
Charred the centuries' bones.

Her Ecclesia met,
By the Baptist river,
Drinking clean water from
Wadi Rum's long quiver.

When the gibbous moon bloomed,
The stars receded back,
And all her former skins
Were no longer stained black.

On the rock's precipice,
The liliest white light,
Grew into her soul's niche
And erased the day's night.

Chapter 1: The Name of Darkness

"Who the fuck are you?" She spat at the man in the shadows.
"I am what you fear the most."
"Thanks for meeting me," she said, acerbically.
"I couldn't wait for you anymore."
"Why is that?"
"I was growing hungry."
She threw a fist full of ruby ash in his face and ran for it.
"You can starve for all I care!"

Cairo, Egypt, Late July 2002

She sat straight up in bed gasping for breath, grasping for recognition of her surroundings. It was already 5:30. *Good,* she thought, better than waking up at two or three and trying to fall back asleep. She had given up coffee in hopes it would decrease the steady fraying of her nerves, but she still had a small amount of caffeine in her blend of oolong and Chinese Gun Powder tea. She set the electric kettle to boil while she took her three-minute shower. When the kettle whistled its urgent scream, she turned off the water, wrapped a towel around herself and set the tea to steep while she dressed. Five minutes later, she, and her tea, were ready to go.

Her black eyes quickly adjusted to the darkness that was subtly fading into day. The wind whipped up from the southwest, scattering a hot dusting of sand across her face. She opened a bobby pin with her teeth to set a few strands of her dark hair to rights. She moved between the buildings and back alleyways as stealthily as the darkness for which she was named- *Khayal.*

She took a long way there this morning. It was important to vary her route, to never develop patterns that could be followed or anticipated. After a few blocks, she entered the mall. The mall was perfect with its security cameras everywhere. She made sure she was seen several times, then slipped into the janitor's closet, hoisted herself up through a ceiling tile and made her way through the ventilation ducts to the rooftop. An easy jump across to the next two buildings and she scaled the fire ladder down to the open second floor window. The safe house was empty at the moment. They left the window open, hoping for squatters, which always provided a good screen. She left the apartment, unlocked, and made her way to the boiler room in the basement. Behind the boiler was a large piece of concrete board. She shifted it aside and crawled through the tunnel, emerging several blocks away in a nondescript office complex.

"*Marhaba*, Khayal," said the man with the radios.

"Good morning." She would only reply in English.

"Huzzaq is waiting for you." He looked up from his work, screwdriver in hand.

"Isn't he always?" she replied. He had been too- since she was a kid.

Khayal

Rounding the hall and entering the travel agency front, Huzzaq said, "I've been waiting for you."

"Yeah, yeah. What is it? Who am I today?" she asked with practiced indifference.

"Which way did you come today?" He ignored her question.

"Through the mall, jumped a couple buildings, then the safe house boiler room."

"I believe you enjoy finding new routes more than anything else."

"I am thorough, as you well know."

"Yes, which is why I have something very special for you today," he said, tossing her a manila envelope of photos and documents.

Khayal scanned the photos, which were of a rug shop. Several more were close ups of a young man, good looking in a slightly less conventional way, perhaps Kurdish, and an older man, clearly related. The photos were largely from the vantage point of the rooftop across the street. Most were of the men, Nur and Ibrahim Al-Wasem, entering and leaving the shop. Only one photograph was fuzzy, covert, taken within the store itself.

Behind the photos was a passport bearing her picture, but the name Noor Al-Hammad. Birthdate: April 4, 1975. Place of birth: Amman, Jordan.

"Funny," Khayal said, rolling her eyes.

Huzzaq laughed heartily. Noor means light in Arabic- quite literally the opposite of Khayal.

"Huzzaq, you know I do not wish to return to Jordan."

"It doesn't matter. You're the only one who can."

"Really? Why not Amin?"

"We need your unique qualifications."

"You mean you need a woman."

"Of course," he answered furtively.

"Tell me then, and make it quick, before I change my mind."

Khayal-now-Noor, went back to the mall to complete this transformation. She purchased a suitcase, the easiest item on the list, and then went about the daunting task of buying bras and feminine clothing. It had been at least a year since she last wore a bra, preferring the tight black tank tops that flattened her small chest under her black uniform or a *chador*. Dressing as a young man or as a covered woman allowed her to move more freely through Cairo, largely unidentifiable.

Khayal

She asked the shopkeeper to size her appropriately and help her pick out shapely, appealing, but not too flirtatious underthings. She suffered the humiliation for expediency.

Noor then toured two women's clothing stores, purchasing dresses, skirts, shirts and two pairs of pants, when she realized her shoes would have to go as well. Much later than she would have wished, she left the mall, suitcase rolling behind her, with the makings of a completely new identity.

Chapter 2: Eight Stones

Noor flew Royal Jordanian Airlines from Cairo to Amman, and took a taxi to a small apartment off the third traffic circle, where a nondescript man allowed her the use of the apartment for the night and handed her an envelope, never once speaking.

She didn't mind. Noor opened the envelope, found a picture of a late model black Saab, keys and registration showing she owned the vehicle, as well as an address in Aqaba and a note that said simply, "You are expected tomorrow."

Well, they didn't say when *tomorrow I am expected,* she thought happily. Often she wondered why she didn't just take the pile of cash and car or whatever else was at her disposal and leave. Go to the US or Australia. Sometimes she thought about waiting until she was assigned to a place she liked, and using the identification already provided, just stay, make the whole visa application process that much easier on herself.

Other times, she wondered why she didn't take her money and buy a new identity. She didn't have that much- maybe $50,000 to show for her whole adult life. But she didn't have expenses either. The other guys took their two or three thousand dollar "commissions" after each assignment and blew it- often literally- up their noses. She just wired the money to her Swiss bank account. No attachments. No needs. Not even a cat to miss her.

She went to bed early, rising an hour before dawn, re-donning her black *chador* to drive to the Dead Sea. The

American kids called the black-veiled women penguins, like Catholic nuns. She hadn't bothered to call them anything at all; she had no friends. While completely unnecessary in Jordan, she liked the anonymity of the *chador*.

She arrived 15 minutes before the sun, paid the small entry fee and tiptoed across the cold sand to the edge of the water. The sun rose behind her, casting its conceited reflection onto the sea. It smelled dead. She sat bundled against the desert night's air, so still one would think her nothing more than a pile of forgotten beach towels.

Noor was small to begin with- a few inches over five feet, 110 pounds of mostly sinew and bone. She did the math in her head. She weighed less than eight stones. She liked the idea of that- eight stones. Even the tiniest of cairns couldn't be made from eight stones, could it? That was insignificant, and so was she.

But this would be different, wouldn't it? For the first time in a long time, she needed to be noticed. She needed one of two men, preferably the younger, if not both, to see her, to become interested, and ultimately attached to her.

The sun had risen and burned the cold off the top layer of sand and the temperature quickly rose. No one was around yet. She stood then, letting the *chador* fall, and stepped into the sea.

She walked as far as she could before her own buoyancy betrayed her, and she could no longer remain upright. She leaned back then, allowing the saltwater to caress her head, cradle her form, and lift her chest, which filled with air and thrust her even higher towards the sky. She stayed that way for a long time. Becoming more comfortable in the water, in her skin, she stretched, exploring her length, letting the saltwater act as an antiseptic. *Enough.* She closed her eyes tightly, dove under the water and swam as many lengths as she could before her lungs screamed; then she burst through the surface in an expulsion of carbon dioxide and hubris, and smiled into the sun.

Noor swam back to shore, walked past her discarded *chador*, and donned her new clothes in the restrooms. She got back in her car and drove south, through the desert, towards the next sea- Aqaba. Pulling onto the King's Highway, she hit "scan" on the radio: Arabic pop, traditional Arabic love songs, Arabic talk radio, and then, the Brit Pop station came in. She paused the scanner to listen to The Cure. The singer said, "...she started smoking poetry." Noor turned it off again. She had no time or patience for such luxuries; she had a job to do.

Chapter 3: Two Left Parentheticals

Huzzaq had taken care of everything as usual. She had a small apartment a few blocks north of King Hussein Street, and only a few blocks from the beach and the Rug Shop. At first, this scared her. She was so used to being untraceable, and now these men, anyone really, would know her patterns, see her in the streets, could- perhaps- even follow her home. But this was the mission.

Noor found the address she was looking for and parked her car nearby. She walked, turquoise suitcase trailing behind her, to a bread shop with a small apartment above and asked for Yasmin. She was greeted warmly and asked to wait a moment by Mohammed, the smoke-scented young man who was kneading dough behind the counter. He returned a moment later with a round, upside-of-middle-aged woman.

"*Marhaba*," she said, shaking her hand and kissing her cheeks. "You must be Noor."

"Yes, it's a pleasure to meet you."

"Come, I'll show you to the apartment and then will make you some coffee."

"Thank you, Auntie." Noor said, using the honorific typically used to show respect to older women.

The landlady led her back out of the baker, and through the very narrow alley to a set of stairs at the back of the shop. Just beyond the stairs was another metal gate, and just beyond that, Noor could see a small garden.

13

Yasmin huffed as she pounded up the metal staircase to the door at the top. She turned the key and used her ample hip to coerce the door into opening. The apartment was plain and cheap, but clean and furnished, exactly the kind of place a single student might rent by the week or the month.

Yasmin showed her the one room space. There were two chairs, a café-sized round table and a day bed tucked into the corner next to a single chest with three drawers. The kitchen area contained a small bar counter, a two-burner stove, a mini-fridge, and precisely two cabinets. On the way to the bathroom was a small closet, which Yasmin opened to show Noor the shelf of two large towels, two small towels, two washcloths, and one set of sheets and then opened the door to the bathroom. It was miniscule, but still contained a bidet, toilet, pedestal sink and triangular shower.

Yasmin walked back towards the front door, handing Noor two keys. "This one is for the door, and this is to the gate to the garden. When you finish unpacking, please come through the gate to the garden and I will have your coffee ready for you."

Noor thanked her, unpacked the meager contents of her suitcase, used the restroom and made the bed before descending the stairs and entering the garden. It was a small and ugly courtyard made of concrete. Dead plants hung dry and crackled from the retaining wall. Pots were filled with cigarette butts in lieu of flowers near the plastic chairs. A discarded child's ride-along toy littered one corner, and ancient rubber bins sat beneath an intricate laundry line that crisscrossed the courtyard, strung with linens and clothes.

Despite the neglect, one silvery-green-leafed olive tree remained tightly gnarled and upright.

Her landlady saw her through the kitchen window in the adjacent building and came out to greet her. "I take in laundry," Yasmin said, waving to the flags of clothes, by way of explanation. "Your rent includes one load per week. More is three *dinar*. Come."

Noor followed her into the ground level of the three-story apartment where Yasmin lived. The dark Arabica coffee was prepared much the same way as the Turkish, with the ground beans boiled straight in with the water and unfiltered. It sat ready on the kitchen table, and two cups in saucers were set.

"Come, come sit, and tell me about yourself," Yasmin instructed.

"Oh, there is not much to tell. I'm taking a break before graduate school to do some independent research in Aqaba."

"You are from Jordan?"

"I was born here, yes, but I grew up in Riyadh," Noor answered, sticking as close to the truth as possible, "and went to college in America."

"New York?" asked Yasmin. Most people knew only a few places in America- New York City, Washington, DC and the state of California being the main three.

"No, I studied marine biology in Florida."

"Oh."

"How long have you lived here?" she asked Yasmin.

"Forever and always," she grinned. "I was born in Aqaba and moved to this apartment 40 years ago with my husband. Since he died, I rent out the apartments upstairs, take in laundry and children. It keeps me from being lonely."

"Do you have children?" Noor hazarded.

"Yes, but my sons all left me, moved to London and the Emirates. They send me pictures of their daughters, but I have never held them."

"I'm sorry."

"No, no, I have my wild children the children of my heart, if not my blood."

"I'm sorry, I don't understand," Noor said, more than a little curious.

"There are so many children here, some have no parents, some whose parents are working or can't take care of them always. I help. I am their *Jaddah*. Nana. Mohommed, whom you met, is one. I got him a job at the bakery. Some wild children are grown up, but still they stay, like Anya, and Nur. You will meet them."

Noor, now having drunk her coffee, made to rise and thank her landlady, when Yasmin's hand shot up and grabbed her wrist. Startled, Noor started to back up, but her landlady exuberantly pulled her back down to sit.

"No, no, you cannot go yet, the grounds are ready."

"Excuse me?" Noor asked, thoroughly puzzled.

"Your coffee is ready."

When she still didn't get it, Yasmin handed Noor back her cup. "Swirl the dregs."

Noor did as she was told.

"Now place the saucer on top of the cup and turn it over."

Yasmin hungrily took the upturned cup and sat still for a few seconds before lifting the saucer, and then pronounced, "Ha! I knew it!"

"I read the dregs, you know," Yasmin explained, scooting her chair uncomfortably closer to Noor's in a burst of three staccato jumps.

"See here," she said, pointing to miniscule flecks that dotted the top of the saucer, "these are the stars. It suggests there is no limit to your potential and ambition. You will be very successful! And here, at the bottom- you see these clumps?" She looked up to see if Noor was paying attention.

Noor was dumbfounded.

"These mean a rocky past. Pieces of your past were very solid, you had a strong foundation; but later, it was broken, and more than once."

"Ah, and here," she pointed to two bean slivers- one right-side up and the other upside down, nestled near each other, like two left parentheticals. "You have two lives within you. One is dark and one is light, *Noor*," she said emphasizing her name.

Noor nearly fainted then. But Yasmin just laughed a hearty smoker's laugh. "Oh pay me no mind. It's just for a bit of fun." She cleared coffee things from the table and set them in the sink with a tonal finality that snapped Noor back into action.

"Okay, well, thank you for the coffee."

"Any time. You are paid through the end of the month. Give me a week's notice if you wish to extend your stay, and come by if you need anything."

"I will, thank you," Noor said as she walked out the door.

"Oh, and just two rules," she called after Noor. "No smoking while the clean laundry is out, and you may have guests, but no parties." Yasmin looked her up and down, ascertaining the likelihood of either. "But if the guest is a man, make sure he's not seen entering alone. Tell Mohammed to come with you if you must, and he'll climb down the back stair case."

"That won't be a problem," Noor assured her.

Chapter 4: Behind the Screen

Armed with nothing more than general directions and a small bag, Noor decided to make use of the last bit of daylight to buy a few groceries and reconnoiter the area. She had almost memorized the map of the town, but her status as a new and temporary resident would make her wandering and photography seem innocuous. She sidled out the alleyway and paused, looking straight ahead into the rug shop, before turning left towards city center and into the long dusk.

Walking past the shop more slowly than usual, pretending to make quick occasional glances at her map, Noor filed information away in her brain. Nur, the younger man, was not there, but his grandfather was. One couple had just left the shop and the old man was rolling and unfurling the pulled back layers of rugs they had viewed. It didn't take long. Surprisingly, there were no yellow carbon copies of sales slips skewered onto the spike, but then, maybe he did the books every day. There were a lot of rugs too; perhaps business wasn't good and the inventory wasn't moving, but it didn't make sense to Noor. It was a huge investment in inventory, but if Huzzaq had a file on them, she could only assume the shop was a front for something else.

She walked on, taking in her surroundings. Cracked sidewalks cradled the *nakheel,* date palms, with their lower bark painted white, tethered to tire strips and stakes to keep them upright, and flame trees with their clustered, crepe myrtle-like magenta blooms. You could tell which side of town you were on by how clean the sidewalk was, or, if there was a sidewalk at all. Noor found a small grocery and picked up a few staples. It was getting late, and she was

19

growing hungry. Noor usually made just a small plate of rice and lentils with *lebneh,* yogurt, or a salad and a piece of fruit, but in the name of reconnaissance she decided to dine out.

Of all rather incongruous things, Noor found a large, two-story Chinese restaurant. Red paper lanterns dotted the nicotine-stained ceiling, dappling the white linen tablecloths with white stars and a rosy haze. Most people didn't eat until eight or nine so it was still early yet for dinner and the restaurant was empty of patrons. The host sat her in the back of an L-shaped room, partially obscured by lacquered wooden screens, for which she was grateful. She could watch anyone who entered without being too obvious. She missed the Chinese restaurants in the US, where she'd order a heaping plate of pork-fried rice; but in Jordan, and most predominantly Muslim countries, pork was not *halal,* permissible. The egg drop soup was wonderful, though.

Noor scooped her soup away from herself, returned the flat-bottomed white spoon to her lips and parted them just slightly to tilt the soup into her delicate mouth. She caught herself doing it, but didn't stop- there was no one there to see her. Had Noor seen a woman eating this way, she'd have known immediately that she was upper class, that she had taken etiquette classes under a tough auntie or her own mother, or that she came from old money. Then there'd be questions. How would a woman of wealth and family be on her own like this? Though not impossible by any means, it would be unusual. Had she run away? Was she in some sort of trouble?

To pretend to be poor then was easier. The anonymity of poverty was the precise cloak that allowed it to continue- a wet wool blanket on a faceless crowd. She felt gross, thinking how convenient the situation, for blending in to one's surroundings. She peeled the cellophane wrapper off the pair of American club crackers, taking far more pleasure in the harsh yet soft crackle of the wrapping than in the eating of the tasteless things.

The door opened and two men sat along the left front wall without waiting for the host to seat them. The host greeted them warmly, but didn't leave menus. One of the diners asked, "What's good today?" But before the host could answer, he said, "No, no, don't tell me. Surprise me! Today I feel like celebrating."

"Very good, sir." And the host went to the kitchen.

Before he came back, five more men had filtered in to the restaurant, pulling up chairs and scooting tables to sit with the first two. There was much exuberant shoulder-cuffing and triple kisses. The men lit cigarettes and puffed out clouds of laughter. The host brought a tray of appetizers, and then the men smoked and ate. Noor couldn't hear much of the conversation, just punctuated words here and there, like a song where you know the refrain, but not the verses. And then two more men joined them.

Nur and the old man came in and the seats at the middle of the tables were immediately vacated and offered to them. The old man smiled but Nur seemed subdued. Another man toasted him, "To Nur, the man of the hour!" and the others followed suit. Nur brushed off their praises and sat back quietly, letting the boisterousness of the others fill in the void.

Behind the Screen

Noor observed them from behind her screen, like a Prophet's wife. Observing but unobserved, Noor felt she had a particular vantage point, a clearer, more truthful picture without being seen, interpreted and categorized. Jubilant men, young to old, were celebrating something. She imagined they had just won a football game, or at least a wager on one. Nur must have scored the winning goal. But there was an underlying sadness, at least a somber note, especially with Nur. And while that many men might celebrate a football game, the odds of these older men playing were slim. No, it was not a football game, Noor determined, and none of the professional teams had played today. She wasn't hungry anymore, but when the waiter came back, she ordered another bowl of soup.

Noor purposefully had not read the files from Huzzaq. He cautioned her many times on this approach- not being fully prepared to meet her target- but, she argued that she needed to observe them first, lest she miss something new with her perception colored by the notes. So she looked at their pictures, but that was it.

Though her view was obscured by the screen, she saw Nur look down, hands in his lap, eyes squinted in concentration. His phone, then. Noor was staring now. He must have felt her and looked up. When their eyes met, she fought her instinct to duck and her desire to never look away. His gaze was like holding a live wire. He said something quietly to the group, and then, "Grandfather, we must go." Noor couldn't say exactly why she felt such emptiness when he left.

Chapter 5: The Target

Back at her apartment, Noor was awake now, alive on adrenaline. She locked the door behind her, retrieved the folder and dumped the contents out on her bed. *Don't look,* she told herself. *Wait until morning.* And then another voice. *You can't wait. You might miss something; look, while it's fresh. Oh hell, she was going to look, how could she not?* The young man's eyes sent electric pulses through her central nervous system.

Nur had a couple of minor arrests on his record. Protesting, border crossing infractions, one speeding ticket, accusations of smuggling against him, but no convictions. Nur Al-Wasem, born in Amman in 1973. According to his license he was 5'11", 175lbs, brown hair, brown eyes.

But they weren't brown really. Noor remembered his eyes boring in to hers. They were dark chestnut, rimmed in amber, like tiger's eye stones. His nose had an angular bridge, the cartilage then flaring out to span the gap left by the rolling plains of his broad cheekbones. His forehead was just a hair too large, but it was softened by the curls that fell a couple of inches. They *were* brown, but also burnished brass from the sun. He kept a short beard that mostly hid the scar above the left side of his jaw.

There was even less in the files than usual. Nothing on the client. Nothing on the old man. No reason he was being watched. Fine, then. She'd watch him for a couple days and then call Huzzaq. No point in rushing.

Noor dropped the scraps of paper and photos back into the folder, sealed it and stuck it underneath her mattress. She went to bed and dreamed.

23

The Target

She was running through a dense jungle, full of hiding things. Something was chasing her. She could hear its feet landing and sliding in the thick undergrowth. The sound of pursuit was a fermata, *almost like ¾ time, with the last beat a rest. Run, run, leap- pause. Run, run, leap - pause. Noor thought it was the tiger, but when she hazarded a backwards glance, all she saw was black shapes, silhouettes, moving towards her. As she listened, she realized it wasn't a jungle at all, just an overgrown olive grove. She faced forward again, but couldn't run anymore. The olive tree was in front of her then. She would've climbed it, but she could barely reach the lowest branch with the tips of her fingers. She turned again, to see the shadows upon her, ready to take her, but now, when she turned, a tiger extended its rough paw down to her. She took it and was launched to the top of the tree canopy. There she was bathed in the light of 10,000 stars, and no shadows could reach her. She turned to thank the tiger, but before she could, he turned to her and said, "Don't move. Stay here until dawn," before crouching and leaping to the forest floor.*

Noor dreamed peacefully the rest of the night. In the morning, she tried not to think it too inauspicious of a sign that her target had infiltrated her dreams.

At 8am, Noor made her breakfast of tea and a croissant, and went out into the garden to sit in the sun. She sipped her tea in the already burning sunlight. Her notebook lay empty before her. It must have been close to 32 degrees Celsius already. The only things that were happy were the olive tree and the sheets, sun-bleaching on the line. Yasmin dragged another large rubber bin of wet sheets out into the courtyard.

"Marhaba (hello)!" she called to Noor.

Noor went to grab the other side of the bin and help.

"Shukrun (thank you)," the woman said as Noor made to grab one end of the sheets and drape them over the line.

"Don't they get dusty?" Noor asked her, nodding towards the sheets.

"Sometimes," Yasmin answered with indifference, "but then I shake them out and take them in to iron with rose water, and no one is the wiser." She smiled.

The two women finished hanging the laundry. Noor hadn't done such a task in years, not since she first left Saudi Arabia. As a student in America, she threw her clothes into a rusty machine with five quarters and then moved them to another rusty machine with three quarters to dry, and packed them in an Army surplus duffel bag without bothering to even fold them. *If I ever have a house*, Noor thought, *I want a laundry line, and a window over the kitchen sink to look out and daydream until the suds have fallen flat again and I pull the drain. The requirements of women!* She laughed. But there was something that made her feel good, and whole, in paying this much attention to something so banal.

"Nur and Anya are coming to dinner tonight," Yasmin stated, looking at Noor to gauge her interest. "You are welcome to come."

"Of course. That would be lovely." Noor was impatiently waiting to meet to Nur, but this was perfect. "Thank you, Auntie."

She finished helping with the line and walked back to her apartment. She had a message from Huzzaq. "Where are you, girl? Call immediately."

Chapter 6: Diving Deep

Noor took a deep breath and called Huzzaq.

"What have you been doing?" he roared.

"I settled in to my apartment and took up crochet," Noor answered him.

"Do not play with me," he commanded.

"What is the problem? I just got here. I watched him last night, and I've been invited to a dinner where he'll be tonight."

"Good," he said, obviously more settled. "But you must make quick progress. We don't have much time."

"I'd make even more progress if I knew what I was looking for…"

"Enough excuses!" he shouted. "Just keep your eyes open," he said, and the phone went dead.

Noor couldn't remember a time when Huzzaq had been like this before, even in the beginning.

Those first two years after Huzzaq got her out of Riyadh, she was almost always accompanied, working for him or the Civil Defense Brigade. There were several branches to the Royal Jordanian Army. The regular soldiers and air force, and Security Defense Forces, who primarily handled the policing activities intrastate, and the small Coast Guard who patrolled the coast along the Red Sea in Aqaba, where she was now. And then there was the Civil Defense Brigade. The Brigade consisted of the firefighters, medics, ambulances and, where Khayal had fit in *unofficially* the Intelligence units.

She had never wanted to work for the military or Huzzaq, but she hadn't any real choice in the matter.

With nothing real to do and feeling that approaching Nur before tonight would be circumspect, Noor gathered her swimsuit and bag and headed to Aqaba.

Rather than hit the public beaches, Noor went to Berenice Beach Resort. Berenice was the old Ptolemaic Greek name for modern Aqaba. For the rather hefty sum of 10 Jordanian *Dinar*, Noor was admitted, given a beach towel, and changed into her swimsuit. On the public beaches, one might see women in full *hijab* or skimpy bikinis, or anything in between. Berenice was more western and after years in conservative Riyadh, Noor felt more comfortable here, with no option of further covering than her rather plain black tank swimsuit.

It had been a long time since she had been diving. She wondered if she still could. Noor kept hovering near the kiosk, debating snorkeling or diving. Finally, she decided she had all day, so she'd save snorkeling for another time. She rented her gear and waited until the next boat was boarding. She took a spot, lined up along the perimeter of the boat with seven others- a French couple, two Jordanian dive instructors, the captain, and two Americans.

The captain didn't take them too far out. They wanted to stay close to the coral reef, but in slightly deeper water- not that the water was all that deep anywhere. For Noor, she just didn't want to have to come up, or float near the surface. Once enthralled with something, she wanted to stay under, absorb it, visit as long as she liked. She was paired up with a fair- skinned blonde woman, who was about her age. They linked a rope between them, loosely held, just to keep an eye on one another. Noor felt if the sweet blonde got in any trouble, Noor could handle it. The other way around and… well, Noor hadn't had any pretenses for a very long time that someone would come to her aid.

Sea urchins dotted the surface of the coral reef, barbed like living medieval maces, and nearly as dangerous. She avoided them as best she could. The blonde pointed to the other side of the boat, and Noor made to follow. Just as the blonde rounded the stern, she kicked wildly, striking both the barnacled bottom of the boat and the reef. There was a fair bit of blood in the water. Noor circled as widely as she could to get the best view of what was going on. She peered beyond the girl and almost dropped her mouthpiece in laughter. There, just in front of her, was an indiscriminately colored puffer fish. The puffer was likely as scared as the blonde.

Diving Deep

Noor took the girl's arm, pointed to the surface and swam with her to the top. She helped her up the slippery ladder and into the boat. She unhooked and shrugged off her oxygen tanks. While the captain was removing the blonde's equipment, Noor had already seized the first aid kit from under the steering column. There was no peroxide or anything, just gauze, Neosporin, Band-Aids and—great— no tape. Noor dipped a bucket into the water and poured it over the girl's leg. When the blood was washed away, she could see it really wasn't so bad. She had skinned her shin in two spots, stretching nearly the full length, and had a puckered hole from a barnacle in the outer side of her calf. The skin of her shin was thin anyway; it would bleed a lot.

Noor took an unopened water bottle and rinsed the areas again. She applied the ointment and wrapped gauze tightly around the length of her lower leg. In the absence of scissors or medical tape, she ripped the gauze with a steady jerk from her teeth and tied the end in a smart granny knot. By the time she had finished, the girl's gear was finally off and all eyes were on Noor.

"Oh, um, I've had EMT training," she explained, and then, turning the attention away from herself, "It's probably fine, but you might want to see a doctor, make sure you don't need an antibiotic later. You never know what's in the water."

"Thank you. It was totally stupid, but I turned the corner and this tiny fish was suddenly a giant helium balloon and inches from my face. I just panicked. I'm sorry."

"Don't worry about it. Are you feeling ok, or do we need to go back?"

Khayal

"No, I'm fine. I'll rest in the shade while you all finish up."

The captain didn't speak much English. He looked at Noor for confirmation. Noor explained to him that the girl was fine, just let her rest. When the others were ready, they could head back.

He nodded and cuffed the girl gently on the shoulder, smiling with sympathy. Noor reattached her gear and hose, sat back on the edge of the rail, and flipped backwards into the water.

Chapter 7: Whatever She Must

Later that afternoon, back at her apartment, Noor spread her marine biology and archaeology books across the small table, just in case anyone were to visit. She pulled the packet of photos back out, studying each one carefully, to see if they held any clues as to what Nur and his grandfather were up to, why she was watching them. She could make no sense of it, and so she replaced the packet under the mattress.

She walked through to Yasmin's courtyard exactly at 7:00, but everyone else was already there. Nur and his grandfather were sitting around the plastic table in the courtyard when Noor walked through. The old man had the ramrod-straight posture of a soldier. Nur rose to greet her.

"Maraca (hello)!" Nur said. "You must be Yasi's new tenant."

"Yes, hello. I am Noor," she said, extending her hand. He grasped her proffered hand, then stepped closer to kiss her cheeks three times. She felt a birdlike trill at the graze of lips on her skin.

"*Jiddo* (grandfather), meet Noor. Noor, this is my grandfather, Ibrahim."

"Pleased to meet you, *ammo* (sir)."

"Noor, what a beautiful name for a beautiful young lady. You remind me of a woman I once knew. Tell me Noor, what is your family name?"

"Al-Hammad."

"Any relation to the Al-Hammads of Irbid?" the old man asked her.

"Hmm, not that I know of, but my family was from Jarash, so it is possible."

"No, no, no. Not Jarash. The Hammads I knew would never leave Irbid."

"Never mind, grandfather," Nur interjected. "Noor is our guest, let's not make her uncomfortable."

Inside, Anya was busy ladling the hot courses into serving dishes while Yasmin was pulling cold dishes from the fridge, handing them to Mohammed to run to the table. Finally, they joined the group outside.

"Ah, Noor, welcome!" Yasmin said. "This is Anya, my sweet adopted daughter!" she added, and kissed Noor's cheek.

Anya smiled and welcomed Noor.

"Come, come. I believe all is ready," Yasmin said, ushering the young women to their seats.

It was still light of course, and hot, but the table was in the shade and the slight breeze blowing through the courtyard made it tolerable. Yasmin fussed over everyone, making sure they tried everything. Noor loved *tabbouleh* (salad) above all else. She'd be happy eating nothing but *tabbouleh* every day, all summer long. Yasmin had made *hummus* (chickpea dip) and *babaganouj* (eggplant dip), grilled chicken and peppers and crispy, salty pan-fried *halloumi* cheese. There was *khubiz arabi* (pita bread) of course, Palestinian olive oil, slices of lemon around the edges of every plate, and a bowl of olives. The logistics of plate passing dominated the first few minutes of conversation, and then it became quiet, until Anya shyly asked Noor what she had done since she'd arrived in Aqaba.

Noor was grateful the question allowed the answer to be kept strictly in the present. She told them of her day scuba diving. Noor was a natural storyteller, an excellent skill if you needed to divert attention from yourself while seemingly talking about yourself quite a bit. Noor made gentle fun of the blonde and the puffer fish, pausing for the appreciative laughter, and largely glossed over her own part in attending to the wounds. Yasmin commented that she had never wanted to try diving. She was happy to wade in the sea when she had time, and she could swim, but the idea of being trapped beneath the water made her chest tighten, and she had to consciously calm her breathing.

"Oh, I agree," Noor said. "I'd never want to go deep sea diving, but we were only three meters down today, easy enough to swim to the surface and the light is still plentiful."

"Nur was a dive instructor in his younger days," Yasmin said, passing the conversational baton to Nur.

"Really?" asked Noor.

"Just for a few summers after school."

"Did you like it?" Noor asked.

"Of course. If I could be in the sun or the sea every day I would."

Ibrahim grumbled something, and Nur stopped him, putting a gentle hand on his.
"I love working at the rug shop now, *Jiddo*," he said, comforting his grandfather.

"And, Noor, where did you learn to dive?" Yasmin asked her.

"In college. We had a P.E. class, just in the swimming pool on campus, but still, you could get course credit and a certification."

"Mmm," Yasmin said noncommittally.

Not knowing what else to say, Noor asked Anya what she did.

"Whatever I must."

Noor waited for her to elaborate.

"I'm a nurse, and I volunteer with the refugees in the camps in Azraq once a month, but mostly at the urban settlement in Maan," Anya said suddenly and made to rise. "Excuse me."

"I'm sorry. Did I say something wrong?" Noor asked when Anya had gone inside.

"No," Yasmin told her. "Anya is very sensitive about refugees. Palestinians who have been here for fifty years are still refugees, though God knows Jordan is much kinder than the rest of the world. She loves her work, but it takes a toll on her. She cannot separate herself from it."

"How could she? How could any of us?" Nur asked with passion.

"Enough." Yasmin raised her hand to quiet Nur, effectively ending the conversation.

"Auntie, there'd be precious little to talk about if we only spoke of pleasant things," Nur said.

Now Ibrahim, who had been lost in thought, became animated again. "The one who knows God most is the one who accepts whatever God has given him."

"You say that to Anya and she may kill you, Jiddo. I don't even think you believe that, for if you did, you would not…"

"Enough!" Yasmin clanked her fork to her plate before Nur could finish. "Go in and check on her."

"Perhaps I should go…" Noor ventured, making to rise.

"No, no, no. You are our guest. I am sorry they are so melancholy tonight. Excuse me a moment. We'll be right back," Yasmin said, following Nur,
Noor was left at the table with Ibrahim, who had resumed his otherworldly inattention, head tilted forward in prayer

or thought, and Mohammed. She hazarded a glance at Mohammed. He shyly smiled at her.

"It is not your fault, Miss," he told her.

"No?"

"Anya lost her baby and it made her mad and then her husband turned away from her."

"What?"

He turned to look inside to see if the others were coming. He could see the three of them arguing through the kitchen window, but could not hear them.

"Auntie says Anya married too young. Her husband said she worked too much, with the sick people in the camps. The baby came four months early- he was too little. She came home from the hospital a few days later, but he did not. For months, Anya only worked and cried. Her husband shouted at her, told her she wasn't dead and he couldn't live in a tomb. He left then. Went to the Emirates for work."

"She told you all this?"

"No, Miss. They lived here with Auntie. I could hear them in the night."

Mohammed was probably about fourteen, too old to comfort like a child, but too young to have witnessed such things. She had the sense that he told her simply to see her reaction, because he didn't know how to feel about it. A levee cracked within Noor; every fiber of her long-stolid being longed to hold this child. Scared now herself, she simply took his hand, lightly squeezing it for a moment. "Would you like to show me around town?" she asked him.

He nodded, eager. "I only work in the morning tomorrow. I can show you after."

"I'd like that," she said and then busied herself stacking the plates.

Yasmin, Anya and Nur returned carrying coffee and desserts, but Noor couldn't wait to leave. She politely sipped a bit of coffee and nibbled a tiny piece of *ma'mool*,(pastry) but claimed a headache as an excuse to leave. Yasmin nudged Anya and Nur.

"Eh, if you'd like, we could show you more of the city sometime," Anya tentatively offered.

'Yes, or Petra," Nur added.

"I'd like that, thank you. But Mohammed already offered to give me a tour tomorrow."

They turned as a group to the shy boy at the end of the table, the one who rarely said anything, but smiled as pure as light. Noor thanked them again for dinner and left, returning to her apartment. She turned off the light in her kitchen but stood and watched them through the window. She curled up in a tight ball, trying not to think, though she could hear them- not what they said, but talking, arguing, in hushed voices through the open window.

Nur rose to leave a few minutes later. She saw him look up at her window, but she couldn't say whether or not he saw her. She went to bed, curled up in a tight ball, and tried not to think.

Chapter 8: Breaking the Fast with an Onion

When she awoke she already had a message from Huzzaq. *Damn it,* she thought. She had completely forgotten why she even went to dinner. *Damn it,* she thought again, realizing she had been handed a perfectly good excuse to spend time with Nur and she had turned him down. She couldn't face these people's pain, not when she had worked so hard to mortar the walls around her own heart.

She called him back, briefly telling him the evening was short, and Nur was inside for much of it. She'd try to spend some more time with him soon. His response was short: "Do it now." *What's his problem?*

Noor got dressed, made a pot of coffee and put it into a thermos. She packed the thermos and three small mugs from her cabinets into a basket. She stopped at the bakery downstairs and purchased half a dozen *girshalleh* (Arabic biscotti) and walked to the rug shop.

Ibrahim was going through a small stack of receipts at his desk, but looked up at her when she entered.

"Marhaba (hello)."

"Sabah el khair, (good morning), Noor."

"Keef halak, ammo (how are you, sir)?" Noor asked.

"Ana bekhair. Winti (I'm fine, and you)?"

41

"Much better this morning. I came to apologize if I upset anyone last night," Noor said.

"You know what they say, 'he fasted for a year and then broke his fast with an onion,'" Ibrahim said, returning to his work.

"Jiddo speaks in riddles," Nur said, coming down from the loft with three rolled rugs perched on one shoulder, under the guidance of a steady arm. His brow already sweating, Nur dropped the rugs on the pile in the middle. Ibrahim laughed, shaking his head and went back to his sums.

"*Sabah el khair*," Nur said to her.

"Good morning," she said, handing him the thermos and *girshalleh.*(biscotti) "I brought some breakfast, and an apology. I did not intend to upset Anya or anyone else last night at dinner."

"It's not your fault. It is we who were rude. But come, have a cup of coffee with me and we'll forget about it."

They sat drinking coffee, and Noor dipped her biscotti into the coffee to warm it and keep from shedding crumbs on the rugs.

"What did your grandfather mean by 'breaking fast with an onion'?" Noor asked him.

"Nothing or everything. It is hard to say whether he is wise or has early-onset dementia." Nur laughed, but not unkindly, and poured more coffee for them both.

"He seems quite lucid to me," Noor added.

"He is. Better with numbers than a computer and strong as an ox." He turned his head to look back at his grandfather. "The onion has many layers. I think he means you have now seen one or two. Whether he means with us or since returning to Jordan, I do not know," Nur concluded. He did not wish to give her the more common interpretation about waiting too long to marry; it seemed entirely too dangerous of a subject.

"Have you lived with your grandfather long?" Noor asked.

"I lived with Yasmin for a while, and then with my grandfather when I turned eighteen."

"Why…" She started to ask why he lived with Yasmin instead of his parents or his grandfather, but stopped herself. "I'm sorry. I did not mean to pry."

"It's ok. My parents died when I was a baby and in those days, my grandfather was away a lot."

"I'm sorry for your loss," Noor responded stiffly.

"And you? Where is your family now?" Nur asked her.

"I have none. My parents also died when I was very young. I went to live with an uncle who lived mostly in Saudi and had little interest in being a parent, so I left at seventeen."

Nur didn't respond, but he was thoughtful. He seemed to want to say or hear more. Noor had always been quiet, by necessity or self-preservation; but now she found herself wanting to talk to Nur. Her words seemed to drift into a cradle of confession, at peace, when she was with him.

"Did you ever see that film "The Little Princess" with Shirley Temple?" she asked him.

He laughed. "No, I don't think so."

"I used to pretend I was her- the little princess- and that my father was injured or away at war, but any minute, as soon as he was able, he'd come through the front door and carry me away."

As soon as the words were out of her mouth, Noor stiffened. She had never told anyone that. She wondered what possessed her to do so now. She could not let herself be lulled into the trap of complacence. Panicked, she hopped up from the rug pile, hastily saying goodbye to Ibrahim, and left the shop.

"*Allah ysalmek (May you have peace),*" Nur said to her back before she disappeared down the street.

Noor walked hurriedly down the wide street, with its white painted palms in the median and careful squares down the sidewalk. She forced herself to slow her pace to avoid attention. *Idiot!* She cursed herself. The mission was to engage him, to make plans to go to Petra or wherever she could to find out more about *him*. In order to do that, she reasoned, she had to give small pieces of information back to keep the dialogue flowing. *That's all it is*, she told herself again. Yet, she was telling him things she had never told anyone. Something in him called to her secret self.

But before she could give it too much thought, Mohammed walked out of the bakery, dusting flour off his shirt. He smiled timidly at her.

"*Salam*, Noor!" he said. "Are you ready to see the city?"

"Sure, thank you," Noor responded, never even making it back to her apartment. It was just as well. She wasn't ready to think.

They walked quietly for a few minutes, while Noor gathered her thoughts. She wanted to be friendly to Mohammed, offer him some kindness, but she also needed to get some information from him to keep Huzzaq happy. Mohammed pointed out his school with the multi-purpose field in front for baseball, lacrosse and football. Even now, some kids were kicking a ball around. They called out to Mohammed. He blushed and excused himself for a moment and ran over to the fence to quiet the boys, returning sheepishly a moment later.

"Friends of yours?" Noor asked teasingly.

"Just some kids I know from school." He hurried her on.

Mohammed was a sweet kid. She rather envied his naiveté, but then, he'd had such a hard life, it didn't seem possible there could be any naiveté left. All the terrible things kids imagine and fear- losing your parents, being abandoned, being a burden on others to raise you- he'd already experienced. He'd heard married people fall apart with the loss of a child, grown children never coming back to see their mother, a woman who was now, in a way, his mother.

He wasn't naïve, she realized, he was just different. She asked him, "How are you always so cheerful?" It felt wrong to ask a 14-year-old such a loaded question.

"I wake up each day to the call of the *muezzin*, prayer call, and I decide, 'I will be happy today,' as the Prophet would like me to be. When customers are sad or unhappy, I smile at them until they smile back, and some of my sadness disappears, too."

"You know, you're pretty smart for a kid," she said, nudging him with her shoulder.

"I have to be," he said, with a grin. "I'm only fairly good looking."

"Oh, very funny," Noor replied. The boy was not quite an Adonis, but he was very handsome.

"If you aren't too old and tired, I'll race you back." Mohammed took off, with the firm belief she would follow. How long had it been since she'd had that kind of faith in another person?

Noor hesitated a moment, looking to see that no one was around, but she could never resist a challenge. Her powerful legs pushed harder to catch up with his gangly ones. Seconds from the bakery, he turned around to find her and she crashed in to him, taking the opportunity to touch the bakery glass before he could get back up.

"I win," she said, reaching a hand down to help him up.

He laughed, took her hand, and jumped up. "Yes, but you cheat."

"You had a head start," Noor panted, "and it's me who cheats?"

"Yes," he said and disappeared inside the bakery with an odd smile on his face.

Noor was pleasantly tired, her feet aching and a small complaint in her back- the kind of minor pain that makes it unbelievably satisfying to lay down. She would sleep well tonight. She had Nur on her mind, and suddenly wished she hadn't been quite so free with Mohammed. She feared he would mistake her attention for something more. *But no, he wouldn't. He's too smart for that,* she told herself. It was too early for bed, so she took a shower, made some tea and went to the courtyard to read.

Chapter 9: The Difference

It was quiet, except for the cars on the streets. But they were muffled by the concrete buildings she was cocooned within, so they produced nothing more than a faint hum, punctuated occasionally, by a horn or the dull metallic reverberations of a loose muffler. It was quiet enough to hear the sunlight fall. What would sunlight sound like? Are light years made of them? If sound travels slower than light, is that why she couldn't hear it? *God, I never understood science,* she laughed at herself, looking at her marine biology books spread out in front of her. At least not the way she should. You'd think that as light from thousands of light years away fell into the Earth, it would make a huge stramash. No, she decided, the sound of sunlight is the same as Christmas tinsel falling on a lush, long pile carpet, heard only by invisible things, like her.

She closed her eyes for a moment to concentrate on the sound. The beaming sun on her skin felt so, so good, and when she closed her eyes all she could see was glowing orange through the thin skin of her eyelids. That is, until a shadow passed in front and her eyes saw the purple of dusk. She opened her eyes, and Nur stood before her, blocking the sun.

"So, you are my shadow," she muttered, squinting up at him.

He moved a bit to the right to block the sun so she could see him better.

"I came to return your thermos and mugs," he said, handing her a bag of her things.

"Oh, I forgot all about them. I could have come by later," she said.

"No, I wanted to see you anyway."

"Really? Why?" She was genuinely curious, and if she admitted it, hopeful, too.

He laughed again. "Do I need a reason?"

"People generally do," she responded flatly.

"Need a reason to see you, or need a reason to do anything?" he asked, amused.

"The latter. I don't think I'm so important that all thoughts revolve around me."

Sitting down and scooting his chair closer, he put his hand over hers. "But you are that important, Noor," he said earnestly.

She laughed derisively. He made her feel comfortable and nervous at the same time. "No, I fulfill a role, a function, like anyone else. And when I've completed it, I'd just as soon be on my way."

"You can't believe that." He looked at her, incredulous.

"And why can't I?"

He hung his head a moment, thinking. "Say there were two bakeries, side by side…"

"That would be a bad marketing plan," she quipped.

He both sighed and smiled at her, frustrated and amused.

"The two bakeries are the same distance from you and their prices are exactly the same. Two brothers own them, and they both use their mother's recipes exactly. Which one do you choose?"

"It doesn't matter. They're the same," she answered impatiently. She pretended her exasperation was with the conversation. Truthfully, she wasn't sure if she was frustrated with him, or Huzzaq, or the whole situation.

"No, no, no, Noor. They are not the same."

"Then how are they different?"

"One is served by a grouchy young man who'd rather be doing anything else. The other is served by Mohammed."

"Then I'd choose to get my bread from Mohammed," she answered.

"Why?"

"I don't know. Because I like him. He's happy and kind."

"But then, even though he serves the same bread, at the same price, he is not just a function?"

"Fine, you win this round, but it's not the same. Mohammed is special."

"Yes, that's what I am trying to tell you. You are…"

But Noor didn't find out what she was because just then Yasmin came out to rule her courtyard.

She stared pointedly at Nur and said, "Ah good, you're here. I need your help inside." As she ushered him unwillingly towards the house, she added, "Please excuse us a moment, Noor."

Noor went back to reading her books, but a few minutes later, a spot of light appeared upon her chest, dancing back and forth in some kind of Morse code. She looked around to see where it came from and saw Nur gesturing, adamantly, towards the courtyard from the kitchen window. He put his arm down and the light disappeared. When he raised his arms again, the light reappeared. *Oh, just his watch reflecting then.* But Noor had the distinct feeling they were talking about her. What she couldn't figure out was what there possibly was to say.

A few minutes later, Nur returned, but his manner was brusque, agitated. Noor wanted to look away, but couldn't. Instead, she saw his face, the man she was supposed to *watch*, but not really *see*. Maybe it was the aging of the equatorial sun, but she didn't recall the creased lines being there before. *Maybe, like anyone else, I only see what I want to see. A target. A single unit, with no context. A job.* But something was weighing on him, literally sitting atop his brow, his eye muscles straining to keep it aloft. Sadness? No, she couldn't wonder what it was. To do so would be to give him context and connections, and it would make her job that much harder. To say something, she said, "If you haven't changed your mind, I would like to see Petra again. Will you take me?"

And as she had hoped, his forehead smoothed out. "Of course. How about Friday?"

"That'd be great."

"Until then…" And he followed the path that led out of the courtyard.

Noor was excited. She told herself it was because Huzzaq would be pleased when she called to tell him.

Chapter 10: Dare Alla Luce

Friday morning, Nur picked her up at 7:00 o'clock in a 1995 Range Rover. It was not the same luxury SUV as newer models, but a truly utilitarian vehicle, with fold out jump seats in the back. Nur's had a well-worn but clean interior. Noor thought of questions to ask on the way, but thought better of it. No sense in putting him ill at ease so early. She intended to look out the window for the two-hour drive, take in the sights she had not seen since she was a girl; but she must have dozed off, coming to when her head gently bumped the window glass.

"Oh! How long was I asleep?" she asked Nur.

"About an hour and half." He smiled at her. "We're almost there."

"Sorry. I didn't sleep well last night."

"No? Anything in particular?" he asked in such a subtle way she almost thought he was flirting.

Yes, she thought. *You. Me. I don't want to do this anymore.* The thoughts came unbidden, and she was surprised at the truth of them. It had been building for some time; she just hadn't realized it before.

"Just the anticipation, I guess," she lied.

Nur knew she was lying, but she said it with such a beautiful smile, he didn't mind the trade-off. "Hmm," was all he said.

They parked near the top, got out and stretched their legs. Nur took a backpack out of the trunk and put a couple bottles of water in it.

The heat of day came with a hot wind that blew hot sand in her still hotter face.

"Shall we walk?" Nur asked, but saw the quick glance Noor made towards the horses. "No, let's ride."

Past the ticket stands and the cheap imitation souvenir sellers, they paid the Bedouin guides and stepped into the stirrups of the horses. Something felt majestic about the long, one-kilometer descent through the narrow fissure in the canyon atop a horse. On both sides, the canyon walls extended three or more stories high. On the left was the tomb of obelisks, on the right, the dam. Water, wind and men had carved the sandstone walls into niches for God, tombs, rivulets, stairs, and soft caverns. The sandstone walls were striated with ochre, rust and even dusky rose quartz. At the outset, they could easily ride abreast, with four or five horses, but by the end of the *siq*, or crack, in the canyon, there was barely enough room for a single rider to pass through. Years ago, Noor had read that *dare alla luce*, "to give birth," in Italian is literally translated as "to give to the light." She was reminded of that now, as the riders were born from the long and narrow cleft and spilled out into the bright, open world of Petra.

Camels kneeled on calloused knees outside the 2000-year-old Treasury. One can tour the city of Petra on camel-back, or pay a few dinar to have a picture taken astride the ruddy jument. Noor did neither, but, greeting the Bedouin man with the camel, asked if she could pet it. She had forgotten how big they really were. Its neck was much larger than a pommel horse, taut, and powerful. Even lying down with its legs folded beneath it, he was almost as tall as Noor. The camel's eyes were like black walnuts, its lashes a series of long honeysuckle stamen as he blinked at her before casually yawning. The camel's yawn is the least graceful thing on earth,: rubbery lips extend, revealing yellowed teeth the size of Legos, and a long pink tongue. You'd laugh, except even when calm and seemingly docile, there's a strength and foreignness to a camel. You can't quite trust them. She patted his neck again, eyes on his all the while, and thanked the Bedouin, handing him an unopened bottle of water.

Nur waited patiently until she came back, then ushered her towards the Treasury. Only the "lobby" can be entered- the rest long since worn away and blocked up. It was remarkably cooler in the antechamber. Noor took her hat off, waving it up at her face as she looked around, stopping here and there to place her palm to the cool stone, closing her eyes, connecting with it. Nur didn't know what to make of it, of her. He leaned against the entrance wall, and waited for her.

"You're always waiting for me," Noor said.

"I don't mind," Nur said.

"No, show me your favorite spots. I'll keep up."

"I'm not sure you can," he said, with a sly grin.

"Are you challenging me? I beat Mohammed in a race the other day."

"I know, but he told me you cheated," Nur laughed.

"I did no such thing. And anyway, what's the challenge?"

"Come, I'll show you."

They walked through the city, as it began to widen past the Facades Street, finally opening completely, revealing the rest of the hidden city. The amphitheater sat on the left and the Silk Tomb on the right. Gazing up at the tombs or rooms, it was impossible to tell which was which anymore, except for the royal tombs- those were obvious. Would it be strange to be buried in the same fashion in which you lived? In a sandstone sarcophagus? Or would it merely be like walking from one room of your life to another, as straight-forward as a hallway? Black soot from fires marred the stone ceilings, and occasionally one could make out the carvings of a small shelf or niche, but there was no other sign of habitation here.

Across the open desert plain sat the Church and restaurants and public buildings. Beyond that, eroding stairs and swift cutbacks in the mountain of sandstone appeared again.

Stopping for tea and water, Nur asked her, "If you had to pick a number between one and a thousand, what would you choose?"

"Hmmm." She made a play of thinking on this, though she already knew her choice. "822, perhaps?" Noor smirked.

"You knew?" he asked, disbelieving.

"You said it was a challenge. There are 822 steps to the top of the monastery. I couldn't think of anything else it would be."

"You're right, of course. It's best to go early morning, but if you're up for it, you should see it."

"Let's do it. But if you pass out, I can't carry you to the top." Noor laughed with bravado and started jogging up the steps, without waiting for Nur to catch up.

"Mohammed was right. You do cheat," he laughed behind her.

"Ha! I learned this trick from him." She turned around to smile at him before continuing up the eroded steps.

Past the Girls Palace and the Fortress, about halfway up near the Winged Lions temple, Nur asked her if she wanted to pause, to rest. She did, of course. The stairs were much like scaling the side of the mountain itself. But she just said, "Nope," and kept going.

Though her pace was much diminished, Noor made sure to stay a few feet ahead of Nur. Any time she felt him start to close the gap, she picked up the pace a hair. It was a matter of pride, but also an occupational habit of staying out of arm's reach.

At the top, Noor fought the temptation to collapse onto the rock face, knowing it would only make her sore later. So she spared only a minute to stare at the monastery before her. Whether it was the presence of a higher power or just the sweet relief of not climbing any more, Noor was moved by the sight. Her limbs felt like they were still moving. When she was a kid, she would push her forearms against the doorframe, exerting all her force for as long as she could stand it. When she stepped out of the doorway, her arms would rise like a hawk's wings, of their own volition. She felt her limbs still moving, climbing an interminable staircase to… what? Heaven? Or a never-ending series of Sisyphean tasks?

Nur was a pile of jelly bones, slumped atop a rock, fishing in his bag for water and a cigarette.

"Really?" she laughed.

"It's only because I train my body to function on so little oxygen that I made it up those stairs," he puffed.

"That makes an odd amount of sense, though I never was very good at science." She said this without thinking and turned to stretch her legs and walk around a bit to cool down.

Returning a few minutes later, she stretched her legs again, pulled one arm above her head and one behind her back, clasping, and then the other way. When she did so, her soft green t-shirt lifted, showing just a little bit of her stomach. Nur was still sitting on the rock, at eye level with her waist, staring. *Damn it*, she thought, quickly dropping her arms and pulling her t-shirt back down.

"Noor, what- " he started to ask.

"Nothing," she said with finality. "Let's go." And she walked into the monastery without waiting for him.

The interior of the monastery was a sacred place, a refuge. Nur would respect that, and there would be no talking. For such a massive structure, again, very little remained accessible. From the outside, it looked like a simpler version of the Treasury. From the inside, it was a carved-out large room, with some crosses and Christian symbols added in the second century to what was, likely, originally another temple or tomb. People make the climb, not so much for the monastery itself but for the views. Noor took the few moments in the cooler interior to collect her thoughts.

Nur walked out before her and stood at the precipice, overlooking the village below. Noor took her time returning to his perch. She took out her camera, but instead of photographing the town below, she captured a Phoenician juniper, twisting like arthritic bones from a small crack on the edge of the mount. It had to be at least a hundred years old, maybe older. The desert breeds small things, diminutive people even, as if the smaller something is, the less water it will require. But of course, the camel makes no sense in this theory.

Juniper, Ziziphus or spinichristi- literally spine of Christ, though many doubt the crown of thorns was made of this- or *nebk*, in Arabic, cinnabar, acacia, thistles, oleander and anemones and dust grow in Petra. Nothing else. Noor turned her camera and pressed the repeat shutter function, surreptitiously taking dozens of photos of Nur, before turning her camera at the monastery's façade.

"We should go if you wish to see the Church on the way back," Nur told her. His demeanor had changed. It was of slight impatience, well-concealed, but as if their interactions had changed strictly back to business.

And what was the business at hand? Noor wondered for the hundredth time. She cursed herself and Huzzaq and all of it. How could she be so careless? That idiotic comment about science? Allowing her shirt to come untucked. It was not that he was shocked by seeing skin. She knew he had seen her skin and her scars. And there was no explaining that. The heat had gotten to her. She couldn't even think of a way out of this.

"Yes, of course." This time she followed him down the craggy steps to the flat open area before the Church. They dodged overheated tourists being led up to the monastery on sturdy donkeys, led by boys no older than ten. *What a miserable existence,* she thought. She felt sorry for the donkeys; at least the boys could understand; it was for money. The donkeys had no idea why they walked up and down 822 steps over and over each day, laden with more than their own weight in milky red tourists. The boys may even grow up and escape this life, move up to hustling middle-aged European women for the scam of love and the art of money. *I've turned into the worst kind of person,* Noor thought, *cynical and barely functional.* It was no wonder, really. It had started with her Uncle Kadir. It continued with Huzzaq. The only times she had known otherwise, she was too young to remember. She couldn't remember anything before the age of seven. Surely that was strange, too.

Her thoughts were interrupted when Nur paused at the entrance of a tomb, talking to the Bedouin sellers, taking shelter from the sun. He asked for tea, and a woman of indeterminate age with a grey ash geometric tattoo on her forehead waved them closer. She poured two cups of hot mint tea and waved those, too, towards them. She leaned back on her haunches, smiling all the while. Noor blew on the tea, taking the tiniest sips from the scorching liquid. What she really wanted was iced water, but the hot tea was better. It tricked the body into cooling down. *What else could the body be tricked into?* she wondered.

The Bedouin woman went back to her embroidery. How the woman could possibly see in the dimness of the cave, or the blinding light of the sun, was beyond Noor. She had a blanket spread out next to her, with small pieces laid out flat. Nur complimented the woman on the small rag dolls she hand-stitched and embroidered with geometric designs, in bold reds and blues. The woman handed Nur a male and female doll holding hands, stitched holding hands forever. She pointed at Nur and Noor and then the two dolls again and laughed. Nur kindly asked how much they cost. The price was absurdly high, but Nur took two larger bills from his pocket and said, "This is what I have to give you, though you most certainly could and should have more."

It was the politest form of bargaining. The woman did not hesitate.

She patted Nur's cheek with her roughened palm. "For you, yes. But you must promise to take care of her," she added.

It was completely unclear to Noor whether she was referring to the doll or to her. Noor thanked the woman for the tea, for which they were never charged.

They stopped at the Church, covered in archaeologists' canvas dome. The aisles went up both sides of the perimeter covered in mosaics of fantastic beasts. The middle was unadorned. Maybe there had been pews here, or prayer mattes most likely. It was beautiful. Noor wanted to stay, but it was crowded and her heart just wasn't in it anymore. She was too worried about Nur, though she told him she was just tired. The day's exertion was reason enough for little conversation on the way back to the car.

Chapter 11: Secret Names

After all her silent stalling, Noor still had no idea what to say once she was back in the car with Nur. *I guess I'll just wing it,* she thought. *React, like I always do.*

It was a good theory, but Nur cut straight to the chase.

"Noor, I couldn't help but notice the scars on your stomach."

Noor sat frozen.

"There were a lot of them. Small and round, like burn marks."

There was nothing she could say.

"Noor, did someone burn you?"

"It's not the kind of thing I'm accustomed to talking about," she snapped.

"No, I wouldn't think so. But you'll forgive me for asking?"

"What, exactly, are you asking?"

"They look like cigar and cigarette burns, Noor. Are they?"

"If that's what they look like, then I suppose they must be," she said flatly, hoping he'd stop talking if she were abrupt and rude enough.

"Who did this to you?" Nur asked.

"It doesn't matter."

"Of course it matters!"

"No, it doesn't. It was a long time ago and he is gone now, anyway."

"Alright," he said to pacify her, and continued driving in silence. Noor started to think this could all be forgotten. They'd move on like it never happened, and she could get back to whatever it was she was meant to do.

He lit a cigarette and cracked the window. She rolled her window down too. He quickly tossed it out the window, where she could see its red cherry bouncing along the highway in the side view mirror.

"I'm sorry. How thoughtless of me," he said.

"It doesn't bother me," Noor replied.

A few minutes passed. He gripped the steering wheel harder, large knuckles turning white. "Noor, how is it that someone who isn't good at science becomes a marine biologist?"

She didn't answer. It was there, on the tip of her tongue-the perfect lie. But she couldn't bring herself to say it to him.

"Noor?" he asked her again, but she still couldn't answer. And yelling now, "Noor, damn it, tell me!"

"Stop calling me that!" she screamed back in frustration.

Nur slammed on the brakes and pulled over onto the sandy shoulder.

"What are you doing?" Noor asked him, scared. She was alone, in the middle of the desert with her target. Nur turned to her.

"Why should I stop calling you Noor?" he demanded.

Noor sat still, outwardly as impassive as stone. The seconds ticked by, in time with her heartbeat. She thought, for a moment, that she could hear his heart, too. Anyone else would have given up, but Nur was immovable.

"Tell me why."

Even stones could be moved. She thought of the Castle at Al Karak. Someone moved those stones. People thought Stonehenge was a time portal. *If rocks and time can be moved*, she thought, *maybe so can I.*

Steeling herself to look at him, she replied quietly, "Because... it's not my name."

"What is your name?" he prodded her.

"Please-"

"I'm not a wizard, Noor, or whoever you are. Telling me your real name won't give me some mystical power over you."

She laughed then. "You say that like it's absurd, but actually, it's pretty close to the truth."

"What is your name?"

"I can't tell you." Her hands trembled.

"Can't or won't?" He smacked the steering wheel and she flinched. "I won't hurt you. You know I'd never do anything to hurt you, right?"

"No. I don't know that. How does anyone ever know that?" she replied in her typically cryptic and cynical manner.

"Close your eyes," he urged her.

She hesitated. She didn't want to. This was against all the rules. Never take your eye off the target. Of course, never divulge anything about yourself was also a rule. He undid his seatbelt and turned to her, placing two hands on the sides of her face. He looked into her eyes, showing her the truth in them. He would not hurt her.

She closed her eyes. He sat there, still, except for his thumb pads caressing the sides of her cheeks, erasing an errant tear until her breath slowed some. He kissed her, slowly, tentatively, giving her every opportunity to pull back. But she didn't move away. She kissed him back with an eagerness bordering on viciousness, pulling him towards her. He gave in, letting her think she was in control for a moment, before gently and slowly pulling back.

"Tell me your name," he said again.

"Khayal," she stated clearly, almost daring him to turn on her. She watched him for any hint of recoil, for any sign he'd take it all back once she had said it, once he had gotten what he wanted.

"There, now I am your *djinn* (genie)," he said. "I'll protect your secrets and your secret name."

She smiled cautiously at him as he put the car back in drive and pulled onto the highway. A moment later he said, "Now I shall have to change my name."

"What do you mean?" she asked.

"You said I am always waiting for you. Perhaps I should be the one called 'shadows'."

She laughed.

"Khayal?"

"Yes?"

"Never lie to me again," he said severely.

It startled her, but the look in her eyes made him soften. "If you can't tell me something, don't answer. Just don't lie to me."

"Then I may be the quietest woman you've ever known." Her feeble attempt at a joke merely earned her a raised eyebrow.

"Okay. Does this pact flow both ways?" she asked.

"Of course."

"What do you do for a living?"

"Exports," he said with a grin and a shrug, pulling back onto the road and speeding even faster down the King's Highway.

"Riiiight," she laughed and rolled the window all the way down to the cooling desert wind.

Chapter 12: Dead Men Tell No Tales

Nur dropped her off in front of her building, but made no move to walk her in or kiss her again. *It's better this way*, she thought. *I'm a wreck, off my game. God knows what I'd do.* She unlocked her door, and locked it again once inside, counting to twenty before going to the window to see if he was still there. His car was already gone.

A moment later, she heard a faint knock at the door. She smiled. He must have changed his mind, went to park the car. She unlocked the bolt and opened the door wide with expectations she was trying not to have.

But it wasn't Nur at all. One of Huzzaq's goons burst in the door. She stifled a scream. He ignored her, walking in to the apartment. She got in front of him.

"What do you want?"

"Where is it?" he bellowed.

"Where is what? What do you want?"

"Give me the file, girl."

"I don't know what you're talking about."

He backhanded her instead of arguing. She held her palm to her stinging face as he started rifling through her drawers, dumping them on the floor.

"Did Huzzaq send you?"

"Ha! Huzzaq is finished."

"Then who sent you?"

"People get hurt when they forget their place, when they fail to complete their missions." He leered at her.

"Get out!" She started throwing books at him, which he ignored as he continued rummaging through her things. As he bent over the mattress, digging beneath, she grabbed the heavy barstool by the legs and hit him over the head with it. He crumpled, face down on the floor. Noor crouched, checked his pulse, and pulled his wallet out of his pants pocket. It was likely an assumed identity, but she had to start somewhere.

She heard another faint tapping on the door, but it was partially open already. A sleepy-headed Mohammed stared, mouth agape at her.

"What-?"

"Mohammed, please shut the door. I'm sorry as hell to ask you this, but can you please get the duct tape from the kitchen? Bottom drawer next to the sink." She rested her knee on the man's kidney in case he moved.

Not knowing what else to do, Mohammed did as he was asked, returning and handing her the tape.

"Noor, what's going on?"

"I don't know. He came in, hit me and started trashing the place," she answered as she put three pieces over his mouth.

"I'll call the police." Mohammed made to move towards the phone.

"No!" she shouted.

The stern tone of her voice caught Mohammed off guard, and he stared at her in fear and disbelief. Noor continued her work, capably ripping the tape with her teeth and winding it around his wrists. "No, I'm sorry, but please do not call the police," she said more softly, taping the goon's ankles together. Then she tied his hands to his feet.

"Are you in some kind of trouble?" Mohammed hesitantly asked her, horrified at the proficiency with which she completed the task.

"Not exactly. But the less attention here, the safer we'll all be."

"What are you going to do with him?"

"Shit. I have no idea," she said, leaning back on her knees and tucking her feet beneath her.

"Well, we can't leave him here."

"Yes, I know. Let me think," she said, distracted.

"I'll be right back," he muttered as he ran down the back stairs.

A moment later, Yasmin appeared with Mohammed on her heels.

"You told her?" Noor accused.

"No, or not at first," Yasmin responded. "I caught him taking the large laundry bins. You know, the ones on rollers?"

"Huh?"

"I thought we could wheel him out in the laundry and no one would suspect even if they did see us," Mohammed explained. "She nearly ripped my ear off!" he added, glancing up at Yasmin.

Noor was torn between shock and amusement.

"Who is he?" Yasmin asked, oddly calm, given the circumstances.

"I don't know," Noor replied.

"Well, what is it you do know?" Yasmin remained serene.

"What are you talking about?" Noor was exhausted and losing patience.

"Yes, you're right of course. No time for that now. We have to get rid of the body," Yasmin said matter-of-factly.

"God. He's not dead!"

"Too bad," Yasmin said, and then, seeing the look of horror on Noor's face added, "Dead men tell no tales," and laughed.

"But they don't tell secrets either," Mohammed pointed out, "and I'd like to know why he did this to Noor."

"Oh, have you two done this before?" Noor asked sarcastically, but the look between Mohammed and Yasmin did not go unnoticed.

"We need to get him somewhere far from here before he wakes up," Yasmin said, "unless you were planning on questioning him?"

"I won't get anything out of him," Noor sighed. "How are we going to get him out of here? He's got to weigh 125 kilos and we can't just roll him down the stairs."

"Don't worry, Nur is on his way," Yasmin assured her.

"WHAT!? You called Nur?" Where Noor was relatively calm a moment ago, the mention of Nur sent her into a panic. She could feel her heart beating outside of her chest, her stomach clenching, bile rising up in her gorge. *What's going to happen when the first man I've ever... when he finds out about this?*

"We can't carry him by ourselves, and I never leave the house late at night- it'd be noticed." Turning to Mohammed, she ordered, "Get the large laundry cart and put it by the back staircase. Get some sheets to put on top."

Before Noor could protest, Nur came in the side door, looked from Yasmin to the motionless man on the floor to Noor's face. Seeing the blossoming bruise on her cheek, he crossed the room in two strides and squeezed her to him. "*Allah* (God)! Are you alright?" He leaned back to look her in the eyes.

"Yes."

"Is *he* alright?" He motioned towards the man on the floor.

"Just unconscious. I hit him over the head with the barstool," Noor explained.

"Okaaaaay. I guess this is going to be one of those *quiet* times?"

She nodded. "For now."

"Enough chatter. Let's get him out of here!" Yasmin barked. "Nur, there's a cart at the bottom of the back stairs. You and Mohammed carry him down and put him in it."

"What are you going to do with him?" Noor asked.

Nur had completely taken charge of the situation. "Dump him outside the city. Let him walk back," Nur said, moving to pick him up.

"Wait-" Noor took his wallet, keys and cell phone, then put tape over his eyes. "I don't want him to know who you are if he wakes up."

They got the man into the laundry cart, piled sheets on top of him. A white commercial van appeared at the end of the alley, and Ibrahim got out and opened the back doors.

"Mother of God! You told Ibrahim?" She stared at Nur.

"Someone has to drive the van. Mohammed is too young," he stated matter-of-factly.

She just stood there shaking her head. They *should be freaking out- not the other way around*, she thought. *What in the hell was wrong with these people?*

She followed the laundry cart to the end of the alley and helped lift it into the back of the van. She went around to the passenger side, but Nur stopped her.

"You can't go," he said.

"It's my mess, I'm pretty sure I should go help dispose of it," she snapped, officially at the end of her tether.

"No, Jiddo and Mohammed will go. We will stay at Yasmin's," he instructed.

"He's a kid. And he's an old man!"

"Exactly. They will not be noticed. You have a black eye that's not exactly inconspicuous. Go to Yasmin's. I'll lock up and be there in a few minutes."

Yasmin led her into the living room and urged her to sit down. "I'll make tea," she said.

"Do you have anything stronger?" Noor asked.

Yasmin just hummed as if she didn't hear her.

Ten minutes later, Noor was on the couch sipping the oddest flavored tea, when Nur returned. She thought she would be awake all night on adrenaline, but all of the hiking at Petra, or maybe shock, made her limbs start to feel like stone. She didn't see Nur look questioningly from the teapot to Yasmin, or Yasmin give the slightest shake of her head. She just felt her eyelids grow weighted with concrete and her fingers pried from the cup as she sank into the sofa. She could hear Nur and Yasmin talking in hushed tones, arguing maybe, but she had the most delightful feeling of detachment about what was going on around her.

She was running, again, through the grove. Heat and humidity wrapped like thick vines around her chest, her throat- suffocating, choking. She was so tired. She couldn't keep running, she was slowing down against her will. She leaned against a large tree, dripping with wild grape vines. A thick paw came around her chest and pulled her into a den, hidden beneath the vines and tree roots. Be quiet, *he said, without speaking. She followed the beast down the dirt tunnel, crawling most of the way until it opened into a borough. It was the unlikeliest of rooms. The floor was*

tamped earth with an oval rag rug covering much of it and a small fireplace in the corner. She stopped and stared.

The man in the corner was ancient and frail, twisted and wraith-thin, like an old olive tree. But when he raised his head, his face was plain.
"What do you want?" she spat.
"Come, child," the frail man whispered, like the last bit of steam from a teapot.
Noor *didn't want to. She knew this man,* she thought she knew this man, *she amended. She stood frozen.*

"I'd come to you, but as you can see…" he said, gesturing to his legs which were no longer there, "I'm not able."

The tiger nudged her towards the old man in the chair before the hearth with the crest of his head.
"Traitor," *she said to the tiger, but he only growled, urgent but not menacing. When she was within his reach, he grabbed for her, but instead of striking or hurting her, he did something far more shocking. He pulled her in to his embrace, arthritic fingers clutching her curls, smoothing them back, with more strength than she would have imagined.*

Noor woke in the early morning, disoriented, thinking that she was hallucinating. Nur held her, half reclined on the sofa. *I should leave*, she thought before the weight of her lids and his arm and everything that had happened pulled her back down and she slept some more.

Chapter 13: Only Two Possibilities- Fate, or Defying Fate

Yasmin gently shook her awake again that afternoon.

"Where is Nur?" Noor asked.

"Where is Nur? Where is Nur? Where is *Noor*?" she laughed. "You want to know where he is, but not where you are. Foolishness…" Yasmin trailed off.

Yasmin was beginning to sound like Jiddo, she thought. "What happened?" Noor asked.

"Which time?" Yasmin laughed again.

Noor sat up slowly, but still her head pounded like a fist to the temple. "What happened to me? I'm gonna be sick." Noor ran to the bathroom faster than she thought possible.

Pressing a cold wet towel to her face, Noor returned to see Yasmin grinning, sitting in obviously feigned nonchalance.

"What?" Noor barked.

"Nothing, dear. We gave you something to sleep. After all you had such a fright last night." Yasmin said.

"Yes, a bit of a beating, attempted abduction and possibly murder… tends to have that effect on *some* people. But where is Nur?"

"Cleaning up," was all she said, patently ignoring Noor's insinuation.

"Cleaning up what?"

"Oh, the usual. Loose ends and such."

Noor racked her brain for memories. Suddenly, they all came flooding back, the details she had been hoping were part of a really bad dream. Knowing he wasn't there sent a fresh wave of fear through her.

"He stayed all night, dear, sitting with you, and left to attend to some business this morning," Yasmin assured her.

"Damn it, what did you give me? My head hurts like hell."

"It's a medicinal blend I made to treat your shock," Yasmin said.

"Ha!" Noor laughed wryly. "Fine, don't tell me. Probably Valium and Vicodin anyway, judging by my headache."

"So, Noor, why are you here?"

"I don't know. What do you mean, here? In Jordan?"

"Oh, I know perfectly well why you're in Jordan. I'm asking if you'll tell me, in your own words, why?"

"Why is anyone where they are?" Noor replied.

"That's simple. There are only two possibilities- fate, or defying fate. We both can be cryptic, Noor." Yasmin studied her for a moment, then leaned forward. "Let me begin with a secret. I know Huzzaq."

Noor's eyes widened momentarily before her careful visage returned. "I need to speak to him."

"It can be arranged..." Yasmin trailed off.

"I hear an 'if' at the end of that sentence. What do you want in return?"

"The same thing I've always wanted. The perfect ending."

"I don't have much money."

"Save your money, Noor. I don't need it. I'll arrange the meeting."

Chapter 14: The Past Not Yet in the Past

Noor left Yasmin's to go back to her apartment. The midafternoon sun in the courtyard was the kind of bright prisoners were tortured with. Her skull pounded from the combination of being hit in the face and drinking Yasmin's spiked tea.

Opening up the apartment door, she was welcomed by its gloom. It was dim, with the blinds still closed. Books, clothes, and things were strewn about the room. She picked the books up and returned them to a neat stack on the table. She replaced the mattress back on the bed, but took the sheets off- she couldn't sleep on something he had touched. She folded her clothes on the bed and then returned them to their drawers in the bureau. She vacuumed and wiped all the surfaces down with diluted bleach, as if she could clean away what had happened here. But restoring order to the apartment brought some calm to her soul. She went to complete the restoration by taking a shower.

After scouring herself in too hot water until the tank ran out, and dressing in the clothes she'd left on the back of the toilet, Noor returned to the main room and opened the blinds. She felt somewhat fresher, the fuzzy halo around her head beginning to dissipate. She opened the blinds and the sun's rays streaked the carpet, illuminating dust particles, and a bloodstain on the brown carpet. *Goddamn it*, she cracked.

Noor had no carpet cleaner, but she mixed up some dish soap and cold water and began scrubbing the stain with an old washcloth. She wet the stain and dabbed at it, wet it again, and pressed the cloth down hard to soak up the liquid. It didn't budge. She began to scrub back and forth, more furiously, until her arms hurt from the tense position. She switched to using her left hand, cursing at the carpet. Tears of rage traced cooling rivulets on her burning face. She wanted all traces of him gone, but she couldn't even undo this one tiny spot. It was hopeless.

There was a tap at the door. Noor sniffled, wiping her eyes on the back of her shirtsleeve.

"Who is it?" she called brusquely.

"It's me," Nur replied.

"Go away," she called from her kneel on the floor.

"If you don't open the door, I will just use my key," he gently antagonized.

She pushed herself up from the floor with a heavy sigh, expelling as much of her frustration as she could. She opened the door but made no move to usher him in.

"Why would Yasmin give you a key to my apartment?" she asked.

"She didn't," he admitted. "I just said that so you'd open the door." He smiled cautiously at her.

"That could have backfired," she leveled at him. "What if I'd said to let yourself in?"

"Then I'd have asked Yasi for the key," he shrugged.

She shook her head at him. "Why are you here?" she asked. But what she meant was, "Why haven't you run away from me?"

"I'm here to take you to dinner," he said.

"Really? Does this seem like a good time for a date?"

"Call it whatever you like. You haven't eaten in 24 hours, so we're going out to eat."

"You're awfully sure of yourself, for someone who shouldn't be sure of me at all."

He ignored this. "Get your shoes."

The restaurant was packed and the noise was bringing her headache back on. Nur didn't even look at the menu. When the waiter came back, he just ordered half a dozen things for both of them. Water and *zataar* bread came out first.

"Eat," he encouraged her. "It will help your headache."

The *khubiz arabi* bread was covered in the deep mossy greens of *zataar,* dried herbs- the thyme, oregano, sumac and sesame seeds mixed with olive oil into a paste that covered the bread. It was an extreme flavor- pungent, piquant, something no one liked the first time they tried it, a taste more acquired than beer. But when acquired, the *zataar* required your attention. It could not be ignored. It was like nothing else.

Nur watched her, without making demands of her, not even requiring a conversation. He sat back and waited, allowing her to come back, to come to him when she was ready. She took several bites, drank some water, and by the time the lentil soup was delivered, she had forgotten to be miserable, and gratefully looked up to thank the waiter. Nur smiled at her.

"You must think I am a terrible person," she said to him, trying to maintain herself.

"You must think I have terrible judgment," he responded.

"Why would I think that?" she asked, confused by his response.

"Why would I choose a terrible person to take out to dinner?" He smiled slightly.

"I don't know. Maybe terrible people make you feel superior. Maybe you have a sick curiosity. Or maybe you have a need to fix them," she said, knowing she was only being mean to beat him to the punch.

He looked a little hurt by this, but changed tactics. "I should be more forthright, so I do not cause you to wonder what my motivations are."

That, she did not see coming. She set her spoon down, leaned back and asked, "Okay, I'll bite. Why?"

"Noor, I don't think I can or should tell you *all* my reasons…"

She interrupted him with a snort and eye roll.

He continued, "… but I want to know you. And I do want to help you."

"Why? You have no idea what you're getting into."

"With you?" he laughed. "Oh, I think I have some idea."

"Do you, now? Since you're being so 'forthright', do you care to share some of these ideas with me, for validation purposes?"

"You're strong, and have been trained, both in combat and triage."

"What?" His knowledge knocked the breath out of her.

"You forget, I worked in Aqaba as a scuba instructor. I asked the boat captain what happened that day, with the tourist's leg. He said you must be a medic, because even a nurse wouldn't have bandaged her that quickly."

"Are you spying on me?" she asked.

He ignored this amusing question. "You also disabled a 300-pound man and bound him, and I know you have stamina because you beat me up those 822 stairs at Petra. Shall I continue?" he smirked.

"By all means..." Noor wanted him to keep talking, because frankly, she had no idea yet how to respond.

"You are Jordanian, but did not grow up in Jordan. You have a, let's say, 'different' name, so clearly you are hiding something in your past. You claim to be a biology student, but have no aptitude for science, and then this man shows up and trashes your apartment and attacks you. So, I can only conclude that, whatever it is in your past, is not, actually, in your past yet. Now, with the training you've received, I cannot believe you are as bad at this as it seems..."

"Hey-"

"... no, Noor, listen. You've slipped up too many times with me. But you've survived this way for some time, so something must be different now. That is what concerns me the most. If I can figure you out, so can whoever's after you."

"Of all the many, many flattering things you've just said about me," Noor shot back drily, "what you still have not explained is the original question. Why?"

"I c-" but he cut himself off, unable to answer.

"No, please tell me. Clearly I'm hiding and lying and I am bad at it, by the way. I'm a danger, a liability. Why would any man want to be involved in that? No, why would *you* want to be involved with me?"

Nur exhaled a shaky sigh. "Do you not know how beautiful you are?" he said wistfully.

90

"Right. That must be it. Guys always go hide the bodies for beautiful women."

"I said I wanted to keep you safe." He looked crestfallen.

"No, you didn't. And even if that were true, it still doesn't answer why."

"I'm in lo-"

But she picked up her fork, clanging it loudly against the plate in the process, and said, "I liked you better when you were lying."

He just laughed, completely exasperated with her. "Just eat," he finally said. "You'll need your strength tomorrow."

"Why?"

"I'll tell you when you're finished eating." He smiled again.

"Are you bribing me, like a child, to eat my dinner?" She was amused, but he was still on shaky ground.

"I'm making a pact with you. I'll tell you in the car."

Nur led her up to her apartment, to make sure no one was there, he told himself, but it wasn't the only reason. He leaned in to kiss her.

"Are you going to tell me yet?" she asked, ducking his kiss. He sighed. "Yasi has arranged a meeting with Huzzaq. Tomorrow. We need to leave by 6am to get there."

"We?"

"I'm driving you."

"I didn't agree-" but he cut her off with a small kiss.

"I know. That's why I didn't ask." He grinned as he walked out the door. "I'll be here at 5:45."

"Jesus Jones," Khayal spat.

"Who is that?" Nur asked her.

"A 90s pop star."

"What does he have to with this?" Nur asked.

"Nothing. I've just been trying not to curse so much."

He laughed despite himself, despite the situation. "Sleep well."

Chapter 15: Hiding in Plain Sight

Her head felt much better in the morning, more like a slight hangover. She dressed with none of the militaristic efficiency she was used to. What does one wear to a rendezvous like this? She didn't even know where they were going. She put on long linen pants with sandals – that she could run in– and a matching linen button-up shirt over a tank top.

Nur arrived at quarter to six, knocking gently at her door.

"You look beautiful," he said.

"So we *are* going back to lying," she mumbled, but smiled.

"No, I believe our agreement was truth or silence, Khayal," he said, drawing out the breathy "kh" in her name.

She shook her head. "Let's go."

They took the King's Highway. People said the Desert Highway was the fastest road north- all flat and straight with nothing but sand to see for hundreds of kilometers. But Nur said no one takes the King's Highway far. There were no checkpoints, nothing to slow them down.

Noor wanted to slow down, and she also wanted time to speed up. What would she even say to Huzzaq?

Three hours later, Nur told her they were close.

"Really? Amman's another hour away," she asked, puzzled.

"We're not going to Amman. We'll meet him at Al Karak."

"Why?"

"I don't know. Yasi arranged it. She had one of her long theories…"

"You mean like leaving the bar together?"

"Huh?"

"You know, if it's a secret relationship, you don't leave a bar together. One person leaves and then the other waits five or ten minutes to join them. But everyone knows this, so it's best just to leave together and let everyone think there is nothing going on because surely you aren't so stupid as to leave together if there were."

"This is why there are no leading women in spy movies," he laughed.

"There are plenty of women spies…" she broke off.

"Ha-ha! I'm sure there are," he said pointedly. "I'm just saying, in a movie, no one would follow the plot line like that."

"That's ridiculous. Sure, there's a time for clandestine operations, but what most people don't see is what's hiding in plain sight."

"You seem to know a lot about this, *Noor*. Is there something you'd like to tell me?" he teased her.

But when she didn't answer, he just said, "I'll take your silence to mean you don't wish to lie to me."

She looked at him then, a single errant tear coming to the surface. "I'm trying," she whispered, too low for him to hear.

They parked the car at Al Karak, the feudal castle at the southern tip of the plateau, and made their way up the winding path to the entrance. He took her hand in his and pulled her bag off her shoulder to carry it himself. He laced his fingers through hers.

Though she made no move to retract her fingers, she asked him what he was doing.

"Hiding in plain sight," he smiled, and she found herself oddly calm in the wake of the approaching storm.

Chapter 16: Al Karak

If he wanted to play the married couple, she'd make it believable. They had no idea where or precisely when Huzzaq would arrive; they just had to wait to be found. Though the fortified city had been around since the Iron Age, most of the remaining architecture was 12th century, with feudal walls three stories high, Crusade-era masonry and the large open town within. The stalls around the perimeter were shops today, just as they had been a thousand years ago. She squeezed his hand and led him into a Dead Sea shop. The small stone room was covered in bottles of Dead Sea products- scrub, mud, lotion- all promising to restore something one had lost. She opened a bottle and held it under Nur's nose. "What do you think of this one?"

"It's fine, dear," he responded. "Though if you wish for mud, I can give you handfuls at home for free," he teased.

"But your mud doesn't smell like lily-of-the-valley, does it?" She purchased a bottle and he obligingly unslung the bag from his shoulder for her to deposit it.

The next shop had small souvenirs of all kinds. There were tiny 10 milliliter bottles of rose oil and sandalwood and myrrh. They were so concentrated, so sickly sweet, she couldn't stand them. The shop boasted just about any product you could imagine made of olive wood. There were trivets, Christmas ornaments, carved boxes, Christian rosaries and Muslim prayer beads. All shapes and manners of spoons were carved of the olive wood, the light and darker grains like marbled meat.

Towards the back of the shop were the loveliest cobalt blue glass cups, bowls and saucers. She lifted a small sugar bowl to see the broken patch beneath where the glass blower snipped the glass off the rod. Each glass piece still contained air bubbles that gave the glass a seeded look. She turned back to the courtyard to hold the bowl up to the light. Each bubble was stuck inside the blue that melts, then suddenly stills, like an insect encased in amber or a dire wolf trapped in a tar pit.

Is this a trap? She wondered again. One moment she was ill at ease and on alert, and the next, she was carried away with the life she could have been living, simply shopping with a man who might love her. The desert air was hot and close in the stone confines, and she knew she should surveille the area better, but Nur said, "Come, if you love the glass, I will show you where the glass blower works."

He led her through the courtyard to what appeared to be a stall, narrow and non-descript, except for the face-melting heat from the stove. The wrinkled man had cheeks like an old time jazz trombone player. He set a large chunk of solid glass to the flame, at the end of a meter-long copper tube. The man turned the melting glass, like cotton candy, swooping and flipping it over just before it could drip off the pipe.

Once he had stretched and uniformly heated the glass, he pulled the copper tube back out of the fire with a long gloved hand and placed his bare lips upon the tube and began to blow, just for a moment and then back into the fire, and out again, and blow, turn, turn, and back into the fire. Noor was mesmerized. She watched the cobalt blue take shape as he spun the tube faster to flare out the glass.

With a pair of tongs, he pinched the lip of the glass, spinning all the while to narrow it back in. A vase. An expert snap of pliers at the end of the tube, and the vase fell away. He rubbed the chipped end with a steel file and dipped it back into the ashes. When he retrieved it from the ash again, he smoothed it with heavy rags, and placed it gently into Noor's hands with a lavish smile.

She could barely hold it, such was the heat still simmering within its pores. Before she hot-potatoed it, the old man took the vase back and set it down on the table before her. She expelled the breath she didn't realize she'd been holding. She was captivated, completely in the moment. Looking down at the seeded glass, she knew she was an air bubble, trapped. The only way out would be to break the stunning glass that had so beautifully captured this moment of air.

She bought the vase. It made her sad, and happy, all at once. She envied the glass its stillness. *Of course it's a trap,* she thought. She was aware of how enraptured she had been with the glass blowing process. She had kept her back to the courtyard, all her senses engaged in the battle of blue flame and silicon dioxide. Huzzaq could have put a gun to her back, and she'd never have seen it coming. The strange thing was, she didn't care anymore. She couldn't remember a time when she had been completely absorbed in something, whisked away with the magic of the moment. All her time was spent analyzing escape routes, next steps, and contingencies. And she knew then, she'd rather die than spend another minute living like that, watching her back.

She looked up, searching for Nur and realized... He was gone.

Chapter 17: Terminal

She walked away as calmly as she could force herself. *Do not run,* she thought. She wanted to run. But where? This was foolish. It was a castle in the middle of the desert. Why did she agree to come here? *It doesn't matter,* she thought. *If I had known this would happen, I would have come anyway. I'm tired of running.*

There was no sense in hiding. If Nur had wandered off, she should wait in the open for him to find her. If he had not, she'd need to be visible to whoever took him. Noor sat down at an open-air café, with her back to the business, scanning the crowd in the middle of the castle as nonchalantly as possible. She should eat, she knew, but ordered only a chai.

She sipped the hot, thin mint water, running through each scenario, waiting for the next thing to come.

A man she had never seen walked purposefully towards her. He displayed no outward threat, so she rose to greet him.

"Cousin," he said, "it's been too long!" He embraced her to kiss her cheeks. His breath on her face was hot and menacing,. "We have him," he whispered before settling into his chair, smiling genuinely at her for the first time.

"So good to see you, cousin," she said straightly. "Do you think I'll have a chance to visit with our cousin Nur this trip."

"It depends," he answered her coolly.

"Oh, I'm sure I could make the time if you could arrange it."

"The thing is, there is so much for you to do while you're here. I don't know if you'll have that time you mentioned." His entire countenance was sinister.

"Remind me of my itinerary?"

"Huzzaq's time has come," he said simply. "I'm glad you'll get a chance to see him before the end." He spoke as if there were nothing at all to his statement.

"Oh, is he ill?" she asked. She knew she shouldn't, but she had to press the point, to make sure.

"Yes, he's been terminal for some time. He just needs assistance tying up some loose ends."

When she didn't respond, he added, "I'm so glad you've come all this way cousin, to help him with his passing."

She sat in silence, weighing her options.

"Tell me, who made the arrangements? I'd like to send a thank you note."

He laughed. "Let's just say you go way back."

"And Nur? I'd love to see him while I'm here."

"That's not possible. You see, he is our assurance." The man got up to leave.

Khayal

"When will I see Huzzaq?" she asked.

The man grasped her hand in his, placing a cell phone and keys in her hand. "Very soon, I'm sure."

Noor looked down to see Nur's car keys in her hand. Fuck.

Chapter 18: One Last Thing…

Noor needed to wait for Huzzaq. They could have taken him, but then why bother with Nur or with her? No, Huzzaq must still be free. She couldn't sit there any longer. She walked the other half of the castle wall stalls. She poked her head into shops, but still didn't see Huzzaq. She started to question her earlier reasoning. Maybe he was gone too, damn him. As she walked back out of the last shop, a small group of older men was just sitting down at the café, talking too loudly, and arguing over the best way to light the *hookah* (tobacco water pipe). And there he was- Huzzaq.

Before she approached, she surveyed the courtyard. The man from earlier was gone. She walked up and sat down at the table next to Huzzaq, her side turned away from him.

"What happened to you?" she whispered.

"There's no time to explain. I need you to trust Nur, Ibrahim and Yasmin."

"Trust them? You sent me here to spy on Nur!"

"No, I didn't; I sent you to find each other."

"What? Why?"

"Khayal. Your uncle. He still lives," the old man croaked.

"He can't," she said, leaning back away in horror from Huzzaq. "I killed him."

"No, you didn't. You hurt him, badly, but he recovered," Huzzaq said.

"Then why am I still alive? Surely he would have killed me the first chance he got."

"You're right. He would have. But I convinced him you were more valuable alive, working for him even."

"How could you do that?"

"Because I was the one closest to him."

"You still work for him?" she spat.

"Worked. Past tense. He finally figured out I was the one undermining his plans."

"Even if this were true, how could you do this to me? How could you lie to me, let me think I killed my own uncle all these years, train me, send me into these situations?"

"It was the only way. I had to make sure you were prepared, able to protect yourself. I had to keep you alive."

"Why? To make me a minion in this game?"

"It was your parents' last request."

Her parents? Her parents were dead. This was too much.

"You knew my parents? If they trusted you so much, why didn't I go live with you when they died, instead of him?" Noor asked.

"He was your uncle. I only worked for him. It would have been strange for you to go to anyone but a blood relative," Huzzaq explained.

"Did my parents work for him, too?"

"No. They refused to, and I think they died for it."

"My parents died in a car accident." She protested once more but her heart was no longer in it. It all made sense now. And the man who came to her apartment also worked for her uncle.

"Yes. But your Great Uncle Kadir had them run off the road. He believed they had evidence against him, so he had their car set on fire, and he became your guardian to keep watch over you in case they had told you anything or had left some evidence with or for you."

"How could you let this happen?" She turned directly towards him now, a single tear escaping. "How could you work for him?"

He grasped her hand under the table.

"I had to. Initially it was desperation. But then I thought I could be a kind of double agent, sending Intel on your uncle to the military, while sending people who needed to escape him to Yasi and Jiddo to be smuggled out. I rationalized all the terrible things I did as 'minimizing' Kadir's destruction. As for you, all my focus went towards keeping you alive. I didn't stop to consider what kind of life it was. I'm sorry. I failed you."

She was quiet for some time. She slowly withdrew her hand from his. "No, I am alive. You did not fail."

"You're alive Khayal, but to get any peace, there's one more thing you must do." Huzzaq spoke with a heavy mix of emotion.

"What?"

"You must die."

Noor blanched, as if he were going to stab her to death on the spot. She didn't move, but all the muscles in her body stood electrified, like taut cordons ready to pounce.

"Do you mean to kill me?" she asked, her voice blasé.

"Of course not. And anyway, I'm finished. I'm not long for this life. We have to fake your death and your uncle must believe it, or he will hunt you anywhere you go."

"OK. And I don't suppose we can just go to the police?" she asked, already knowing the answer.

"I don't know how many are on his pay, or if they'll help you disappear, or if they wouldn't just arrest the both of us and get us out of his way."

"So, what do we do?" Noor asked.

"I don't know yet."

"Huzzaq, I have to tell you something."

"There's no time. Go, act as though nothing has changed. I'll get in touch with you soon."

"But…"

Another man approached, and Huzzaq whispered urgently, "Go!"

Chapter 19: Love- Nothing Else Could Hurt So Much

Speeding back down the King's Highway towards Aqaba, alone this time, Noor drove in a fog. The road was too curved and windy. She needed to get out of there fast. She took the Route 50 crossroad over to the Desert Highway and floored it, making it back to Aqaba in just over two hours.

She parked Nur's car in front of the bakery and stormed into the courtyard looking for Yasmin. Immediately, she knew something was wrong. There was no wash hanging out on the line, and the air was calm. Still, she banged on the door, and called out to Yasmin. Knowing it would be futile, like everything else, she turned the door handle. It was locked.

Noor made her way towards her apartment's back stairs. From the darkness, she didn't notice the small hand reach out to her, grabbing her leg. She nearly fell.

"Shh. It's me," he whispered.

"Mohammed?"

He came out from behind the stairs. "Come," he whispered, leading her away from the apartment.

She followed his crouching form from shadow to shadow, like a frog jumping lily pads of darkness, through the alley.

She was almost out of breath when he turned to her. "Hurry."

He showed her to a cellar door, a crawl space really. "Follow me."

Her eyes had adjusted to the darkness outside, but it was nothing like inside the crawl space. It was pitch black. She ignored the scurrying around her, crawling after Mohammed, through the blind tunnel. There was gravel, and she was pretty sure she grasped rat droppings. *Just keep moving* she silently urged herself.

When she couldn't bear much more, she felt Mohammed stop in front of her. He tapped on a metal grate, which was promptly removed from the other side.

"Where are we?" she asked him.

"At Anya's safe house."

They climbed out of the grate to see a worried looking Anya.

Noor was relieved to see her, but all relief melted when Anya turned on her. "What have you done?"

"What?"

"Where is Nur?"

"He was taken."

"And they let you go?" she snorted.

112

"Yes. Where's Yasi?"

"Jiddo came for her. All he said was we were to help you if you came back. What do they want from you?"

"I don't know," Noor lied.

"Then help yourself," Anya yelled at her. "You can sleep here tonight. Then just go."

Mohammed pulled together some sheets and a pillow and tucked Noor in. He was so grown up, a man already.

"She doesn't mean it, you know," he whispered.

"Oh, I'm pretty sure she does," Noor said.

"She's just worried she'll lose more of her family."

"Me too, *habibi* (baby)," she said, gently patting his face.

She fell asleep, but sleep goes as quickly as it comes. Sometime in the early predawn, she awoke, thinking. Taking inventory of her assets.

What do I have? Nothing. Not even Nur. But she had to get him back. Okay, then. *Surely I have something? A gun.* That was some small solace. Mohammed. Yasi and Jiddo were gone, but they might come back. Or not. But she had experience. She could do this again.

In the morning, Noor awoke to the sound of Mohammed and Anya arguing about her.

"Good morning," Noor announced her presence. "Don't fret, Anya," she said kindly. "I'll be on my way."

"Wait- Noor, you don't have to go," Anya forced herself to say.
Noor's heart melted a bit, knowing what it took Anya to reach across that divide.

"Thank you, but no, I don't want to put you in any additional danger." Noor picked up her bag to leave.

"Tell her," Mohammed whispered urgently.

Anya looked torn, nervously chewing a fingernail. She looked from Mohammed's face to Noor's, deciding.

"Anya, if you know something that can help me get Nur back, tell me and I promise you I will get him." She added under her breath, "Or I'll die trying."

"Do you love him?" Anya asked.

Noor stood still for a moment, considered all the things she could say, how Anya might interpret them and if she would help her or not, depending on the answer.

"It's not a hard question." Anya became impatient.

"I spent the last ten years with no attachments, burying anything that resembled feeling. I've never even had a cat. In the last month, I've seen the love of a mother, a son," she glanced at Mohammed, "a grandfather, a sister," she said, looking pointedly at Anya, "but still, I thought only of the love of family. Until they took Nur…"

"And now? How do you know it's love?" Anya asked her.

"Because…" Distraught, she stopped thinking and just answered. "Nothing else could hurt this much."

Anya nodded, decided at last. "There is a place, known to my family, and few others. I think it's where Jiddo and Yasi will go…"

Noor fiercely hugged Anya, who uncomfortably pulled away. Noor just pulled her into a tighter embrace. As she looked over Anya's shoulder, she saw Mohammed quickly drop his wide smile into a countenance of feigned neutrality. But his smile continued to shine through his eyes. When Noor finally released her, Anya announced they'd stay today, gather supplies and leave tomorrow morning.

"Mohammed, take Noor to her apartment to pack what she needs. Leave anything else at Yasi's," Anya directed.

As Mohammed led Noor to the front door, Anya added, "And you might as well tell her. I know you've been dying to anyway."

Noor glanced at Mohammed, puzzled, but he just grinned and led the way.

★

Once inside the apartment, Noor stared Mohammed down. "Spill it," she commanded, and she began packing up her stuff.

"They've all been waiting for you."

"Waiting for me to what?" Noor asked.

"To come here, of course."

Noor just stared at him.

"Yasi and Huzzaq, Nur, Jiddo, all of us," he grinned.

"Explain!"

"Yasi, Huzzaq and Jiddo Ibrahim, your parents- they were all friends. Your parents went off and got married, but both Jiddo and Huzzaq fell in love with Yasi. Jiddo loved his friends and wanted them to be happy, more than he wanted happiness for himself. So he left and joined the army."

"He just gave up?" Noor asked.

"I don't think so. I think Jiddo believed if he did the honorable thing and stepped away, they would get tired of each other, or Yasi would realize she loved him more."

"Did she love Jiddo more?" she asked. "Why am I asking a teenager these things?"

"Because I am nearly as wise as I am good looking." Mohammed smirked.

"Yes, yes, it's true, all of it." She teased him back. "But do you think she really loved Huzzaq more?"

I don't know. Maybe. All I know is she and Huzzaq were to be married, 25 years ago, or something. Forever ago. But Yasi's parents had money and didn't approve of Huzzaq, who was poor and Palestinian, too. Either one, they may have overlooked, but not both. So Huzzaq went to Saudi to try to make his fortune, prove to her parents he would be able to provide for her. Something happened. For a long time, he couldn't make any money, then suddenly he started sending Yasi tons of money, enough to buy this apartment."

Noor thought about it for a moment. That must have been when Huzzaq started working for her uncle. If they had all been friends, he would have met Kadir at some point, and when he grew desperate for money in Riyadh, he went to the one person he had any connection to- his friend's uncle. It was all starting to make sense.

"But Yasi said her husband left her this building…'" Noor questioned.

"Yasi believes what she wants. She has always thought of him as her husband, as she thinks of us- even the ones who left- as her kids; but no, they were never married. He was to come home, but there was always a reason, one more thing he had to do. Eventually they both accepted that there

117

would always be one more thing he had to do. He never came home, but he would secretly send things to Yasi."

"What kinds of things?"

"Money, gifts, people."

"People!"

"You haven't figured it out yet?" He laughed.

"Obviously not."

"Jiddo's business. Huzzaq would send people to Yasi and she and Jiddo would smuggle them out of the country, using either his military contacts or the rug shop. What did Nur tell you he did?"

"Exports," she said, exasperated.

His laughter echoed around the tiny apartment. *Shit*. Noor muttered to herself. No wonder they were completely unfazed by getting rid of that intruder. They did this all the time.

"And Anya? She's involved too?"

"That's why her husband left. She blamed herself for the child's death, and he did too. He thought if she hadn't been working so hard in the refugee camps, sneaking through border control, she wouldn't have been so stressed and wouldn't have lost the baby."

"I understand," Noor said. "I'm not sure why they'd tell a kid all this-" she threw a jacket at him while she packed, " but I get it. Just one last question though- who is Nur to Anya?"

Chapter 20: Wadi Rum, The Valley of the Moon

The next morning, before the first light, when Bedouin fires still smoldered, Anya drove Noor to Wadi Rum, the Valley of the Moon, in Nur's Range Rover. Mohammed had protested being left behind and upon reflection, Anya declared him going a good idea, though Noor couldn't see why.

It felt strange to Noor to be in his car without him. It smelled like Nur- myrrh and a trace of stale smoke, and chai with mint. The car didn't smell too much like smoke- he didn't smoke that much- but this morning, in its confines, Noor felt the air was too close, suffocating, and she rolled the window down. The last time she had driven the Desert Highway was just a couple days ago, but it seemed much longer since she had returned without Nur. She felt Anya's glance monitoring her, her reactions.

"I'm fine." Noor answered the unasked question and Anya nodded.

"We'll get there just after dawn. We could loop around to the north and then approach from the east," Anya said, "but I want to make sure we're seen."

"Are there many people around at this hour?" Noor asked.

"A few. It's best to tour at dawn or late in the day. There are several camps near the visitor's center, but only one remote camp to the south."

"How do you know where the Bedouin camps are? Don't they move?"

"Not Bedouin camps- tourist camps. They pay for the 'authentic' experience of staying in a Bedouin camp and then take a jeep tour about an hour after dawn." Mohammed, who had been sleeping, woke up and laughed at this, but Anya continued. "We'll stop, buy tickets and breakfast, and then drive out into the desert."

"And why would we *want* to be seen?" Noor asked.

"It takes considerable effort not to be seen or heard in the desert. Have you noticed how quiet it is? How many stars you can see? There's no artificial light here. No animals or machines. All you can see are the Bedouin fires. The tours though, they drive all around the dunes, and stop at the sandstone formations for tourists to get out and rock climb. I intend for us to look like one of the tours." She tossed a backwards glance toward the bag in the seat next to Mohammed. "Now."

Mohammed took two *kaffiyeh* (the traditional red-and-white-checkered Jordanian headdress) out of the bag. He arranged one on Anya's head while she drove, securing it with the black-coiled rope called *agal*. He then arranged his own.

"I don't get one?" Noor asked.

"No, yours doesn't matter. The guides are usually men. They'll leave us alone if they think we already have one. Mohammed is too young, but I'll stand back and pretend he's assisting me."

Noor had thought nothing of it this morning, but the fact that Anya was wearing a *dishdasheh* (men's dress) and *jallabieh,* (traditional ankle length tunic), now made more sense- it was easier to hide her shape, and perhaps, be mistaken for a man.

The *wadi* (valley) was the largest in all of Jordan, a great valley carved into the highest peaks of sandstone and granite formations. Wadi Rum was famous for its 2,000-year-old Proto-Arabic Thamudic glyphs, and those of a more recent graffiti nature. It was also famous for its views. From the highest peak, on a clear day, you could see from the Red Sea to the Saudi border.

When they arrived at the visitor's center, Anya sent Mohammed off to purchase the entrance ticket. When he returned, he brought a small breakfast for them of *ftayer,* the tiny triangle shaped pastries filled with *jibneh* (cheese), and *sabanekh,* (spinach), *fuul,* (mashed fava beans with lemon), and a ring of bread with sesame seeds called *kaak.* Noor ate quickly, impatient to be on their way. Anya took the bread in the car for later, and drove them out across the expansive red sand desert.

Anya drove like a lunatic. She gained so much speed over the flatter expanses, never slowing as they approached a dune, that Noor thought they'd crash head on into the dunes. At the last moment, Anya turned the wheel slightly to the left and climbed the dune at a 45-degree angle, dropping the transmission into second gear as the speed they had built up began to wane towards the top. Cresting a particularly wide- ridged dune, like a dragon's back, she sailed the car down the ridge, spinning donuts at the base before increasing speed away from the other cars and heading south. Noor held the roof handle with one hand, and braced herself on the dash with the other.

"What the hell was that for?" she yelled at Anya.

"All part of the tour," Anya replied nonchalantly.

Invincible teenage laughter came from the backseat, and Noor rounded on Mohammed, who was bouncing happily along, only occasionally bumping his head on the roof.

"Put your seatbelt on!" she yelled at him.

"Can't," he grinned. "There isn't one."

Noor turned back around, noticing the other crazy tire paths through the sand.

"What happens if you get stuck?" Noor asked.

"You wait, until another driver or Bedouin finds you."

Mohammed chimed in again. "Once Jiddo took me here and the car broke down just as we spotted a sandstorm in the distance."

He could not have looked more thrilled.

"What did Jiddo do?"

"He just sat, not speaking, until a Bedouin man came on a camel and offered to take us to his camp. Jiddo laughed and replied 'if the wind blows, ride it.' He has a saying for everything. So we went and sat inside the men's tent, filled with carpets. The women had finished cooking before the wind put the fires out. It was a special feast, and they offered Jiddo the tongue and eyes of the camel!"

"It must have been a special occasion," Noor replied. It's very rare that a camel would be killed. "Was there a wedding?"

"No, just this camel was very old and couldn't walk well any more. But then they gave us *shaneeneh*!" he said with disgust.

"Then what happened?" Noor asked.

"I gave mine to Jiddo when no one was looking," he grinned, quite proud of himself.

Noor wasn't surprised. *Shaneeneh* tasted like milk that had been in the sun for several days and then salted, which is pretty much how it is made. "No, what happened with the car?"

"We went back the next day and waited for a truck to come and pull us out," he shrugged.

She rolled her eyes. It had been at least fifteen minutes since they had seen the telltale signs of dust from any other cars. Anya circled the base of a sandstone formation and when she was confident no one else was around, she parked the Range Rover in the partial shade on the western side and got out. She opened the back and grabbed two backpacks, a large duffel bag, two long coils of climbing rope and carabineers. She tossed the first to Mohammed, and the two women waited at the base while he scrambled to the top.

The gear wasn't strictly necessary. The side of the formation was steep but no more than 30 degrees. Anya handed Mohammed a pair of gloves. There was plenty of purchase for his feet, except in a few spots where he needed to use his hands to pull himself up and over to the right.

A few moments later, Mohammed disappeared over the top of a large boulder, jutting out from the side of the formation, and just a minute after that, two lengths of rope, like a pulley, fell from the place behind the boulder.

Anya looped the rope through a hook cleverly hidden behind a rock and attached the duffel bag and backpacks. "Give me a hand, will you?" she said and began tugging down on one side of the rope. Presumably, Mohammed was doing the same on the other because the bags quickly rose into the air and up over the boulder.

"Your turn," Anya said.

"Aren't you coming?" Noor asked.

"I'll keep a look out. If anyone approaches, I'll honk the horn."

Anya secured a seat of rope around Noor's waist and legs. Noor didn't think she'd need it, but it was reassuring to have if she did slip.

Noor found the going to be a little tougher than
Mohammed made it look. She took her time and kept three
points on the rock face. She was moving well, if slowly,
until she got to the boulder and couldn't find a way around
it. She called out softly to Mohammed, asking for direction.

"Halfway up on the right side of the boulder is a ledge. You
can't reach it with your arm- use your leg."

She did. Then she was glued to the rock with one leg half in
the air like a dog at a fire hydrant. "Now what?"

"Put your left hand as far to the right of your body as you
can and push up. Just above the foothold, you can grab the
ledge and pull up."

Noor had been so careful with her three points down, but
this required taking both a hand and a foot off at once. She
breathed deeply and pushed while sliding her hand up until
she felt the ledge. She had it. She exhaled.

"Now reach over to the right again with your left hand,"
Mohammed instructed. He caught her hand and pulled her
the rest of the way up.

There was a narrow fissure in the rock, enough for a person
to slip through sideways. Mohammed took her hand in one
and a flashlight in the other and led her down the *siq*
(crack.) It was only about fifteen feet before it opened up
into a small vestibule, but the darkness had made it seem
indefinite. At the end of the cave was another boulder and
behind it, a metal door with an intercom. He pressed the
button and the intercom clicked on, but no one spoke.

"Open sesame?" Noor joked.

"Don't be ridiculous," Mohammed said, and then, into the intercom, he whispered, "Mellon." The lock clicked open.

"Mellon? Now who is ridiculous?" Noor asked.

"It means 'friend' in…" Mohammed explained.

"Elvish. I know. I've read Tolkien- 'speak friend and enter.'" She shook her head.

Once inside, Noor found herself in a 1950s-era bunker.

"What is this place?" Noor asked.

She saw Huzzaq get up from a chair in the corner. "Secret operations outpost built after the First Arab-Israeli War in 1948." He hobbled over to her and added, "And where I spent some time during the June War in 1967."

"How could this have been an operations outpost? It's solid rock! You probably can't even get a short wave signal in here."

Huzzaq laughed. "Yes, I spent most of the six days trying to get the radios to work! Obviously it wasn't a good Intel post, so it was redesigned to hide," he concluded.

"Hide what?" Noor asked warily.

"You," he laughed again, making her uneasy. "Me. People, those your uncle suspected of spying on him, giving up Intel to the military. It hasn't been used since The Gulf War in 1991. Or, at least not by anyone other than us."

There was always that danger, that someone else knew, wasn't there? Noor thought.

Yasmin opened a door on the opposite side of the room from where Mohammed and Noor had come in.

"How did you get in here?" asked Noor.

"I walked. Up the stairs," she said, two fingers making a walking motion as if Noor were terribly slow.

"Why in the hell did you make me climb over those boulders when there's another way in?"

"The tunnel is too far. No time," Huzzaq answered. "Listen, Yasi filled me in. I have to ask you, besides not telling me they took Nur, is there anything else you're not telling me?"

"Huzzaq, what is my uncle doing?" she asked. She couldn't think about anything else until she understood this.

"What he's always done," Yasmin jumped in.

"Extortion, murder, anything to support his need for power and money."

Noor thought about this for a minute. She didn't want to tell Huzzaq about the demand for his life, but she didn't see any other way. Even if she tried to arrange a prisoner exchange, and assuming she could trust her uncle's men, which she could not, there were too many variables, too many things that could go wrong and get them all killed.

"Khayal, is there anything else I need to know?" Huzzaq asked her again.

"Kadir wants you dead."

"We know that, dear," Yasmin answered.

"He wants me to kill you," Noor added.

"Well, we can't have that, now can we?" Yasmin giggled.

Noor looked at her, baffled by the woman's complete lack of concern. "This isn't funny. I don't know what to do." *These people are crazy*, Noor thought again.

"Can we assume you do not wish to kill me?" Huzzaq asked.

"Believe me, I've thought about it!" Noor replied drily. "But, no I do not."

"We've arranged to put out word that a tourist fitting your description was killed in a scuba accident off the coast of Aqaba yesterday. You should be dead in the paper this morning."

"If I'm dead, how will I get Nur back? Besides, do you really think my uncle will believe that?"

"Kadir told me to kill you," Huzzaq nodded gravely. "That's the price of my life."

"You know he's only hoping we all kill each other and save him from having to do it."

"I'm counting on that."

"What are you going to do?" She eyed him skeptically.

"Well, had I known you were going to kill me, I'd have had word go out that we both drowned yesterday. But it's too late now. I'll have to go to him now, and ask him to keep his word."

"Yeah. That's a good plan," she said with unveiled sarcasm.

"Don't worry, Noor. I'll see this righted."

"Don't call me Noor, Huzzaq. The irony has lost what little humor it had."

"Tell her," Yasmin prodded.

"Tell me what?" Noor was tired of surprises. Surprises for her usually involved someone being dead, nearly dead, or soon-to-be dead.

"Noor *is* your real name. The identity I gave you, it's your real identity. It's who you always were. No more hiding, Noor. I wasn't lying when I told you this would be your last mission, the last time."

Noor wasn't sure she had heard correctly. Her skin felt too tight for her bones, her ribcage too small for her lungs to breathe. "What? What the hell do you mean?"

"Stay here. Don't let anyone see you. I've got to get back to Kadir." He looked at her sadly, touched her cheek briefly in goodbye.

"Huzzaq, wait-"

"I can't. There's no time."

Chapter 21: A Line Once Crossed

They sent Mohammed and Anya back home but kept the duffel bag of supplies. Deprived of Huzzaq to answer her questions, Noor turned to Yasmin. "Tell me everything. Now!"

It was like Huzzaq said. Khayal had been born Noor. When she was no more than a year old, and she started throwing tantrums, her parents began calling her "*Khayal*," the Arabic word for "shadows". It was their pet name for their daughter's tempest moods.

She was an independent and adamant child. Noor had an incredibly long attention span, which she had used to both learn to read and speak early, but also to focus on getting what she wanted. When she didn't, she spent hours in her room, with the lights off, in a self-imposed exile. When she re-emerged calmer, hours later, her father would jokingly say, "She's returned to the light," and pick up his precious daughter. And that's how she got the nickname "*Khayal*."

Everything Noor thought she knew was a lie. She had never even known her real name. She couldn't remember her parents, or a time before she went to live with her father's uncle. Although, now having heard this story, she thought she vaguely remembered a man with a mustache picking her up and swinging her in his arms, and tickling her neck with his kisses. But maybe she was making that up because she wished for it to be true.

Of all the lies Huzzaq had told her, the one she hated the most was that she had killed her uncle. If she hadn't believed that, she never would have done any of the other "jobs." Murder was a line that, once crossed, couldn't be re-crossed; you could never undo murder. You could save a thousand lives, and you'd still be a murderer.

But wasn't that what Huzzaq was trying to do? Take her back to the moment she had become a murderer and give her back her life before that had happened? Was that possible? Had she killed the others? She had long believed she had, but what if it was all a ruse? What if they were rubber bullets? They were bad men, and she had helped Huzzaq cut them off at their knees. But it was only wishful thinking to hope her soul could come back into the light.

Her parents had known Yasmin and Huzzaq and Jiddo. They were her unofficial godparents. But her parents had died before they had made any legal agreement, and her only living blood relative had seized the chance to take her. And no wonder- her uncle had carried an insurance policy on her parents. As her guardian, he could take the money without the same suspicion as if he had been the beneficiary. So he took Khayal, and plunged her into darkness.

Noor had gone to lie down. It was all too much. Tears burned paths down her cheeks and she slipped into the recess of a memory-dream.

Noor told her uncle no. He wanted her to marry one of his business associates. An old man, like himself. She refused.

134

He hit her. No matter; he always hit her. He put his cigar out on her stomach. He was careful. It was always where no one would see. She smelled the stench of taut youthful skin burning but did not move. He'd do it again if she moved. So she retreated to the shadows of her mind, disengaging from all that surrounded her.

She touched the puckered scars, about the size of an American nickel, and cried again until she fell back asleep.

He did it again. Uncle Kadir told her he'd use her so no one else would have her. Let his men use her. Unless. Always an unless. Unless she agreed to marry. No man will have me anyway, she roared, not with what you've done to me! He hit her again. He punched her in the stomach. When she doubled over, he grabbed her hair and yanked her to her knees. She didn't know for sure what he would do, but she could guess. She made a show of capitulating. Cried on the floor and kissed his feet, begging for mercy, forgiveness, for being so ungrateful. She would marry this man. Satisfied, he kicked her once more and left the room.

That night, Noor thought about it. If she married this man, she'd be just as beholden to him. He could burn her and rape her and kick her whenever he pleased. Not all men are like that, she tried to tell herself. But the ones who knew Kadir certainly were.

She got up in the night, tip-toed from her room. She went down stairs and found the sleeping pills he sometimes used. She crushed them and put them in his drink. He was already drunk; maybe he wouldn't notice. But he had heard her come downstairs and was suspicious and followed her. What have you done? He charged into the room. I've only come to make you a drink, Uncle. He took the drink in one gulp. He tasted something, too late. He backhanded her and she spun around but did not fall. The bottle was still in her hand. Without thinking, she charged at him, broke the bottle over his head. As he stumbled, she plunged the broken bottle into his lower back, into his right kidney. She would never have been able to do this, but he was slowed already by the drink and by the drug.

The memories came to her in bits and pieces. There was blood everywhere. So much blood. Huzzaq came in. "Yalla! Girl, we must get you away from here." She feared him, too because he worked for Kadir. She pulled the bottleneck out of Kadir's back and waived it at Huzzaq. "I will not be made a whore or a wife!" she screamed. "I know," he said. She had no other choices, so she dropped the bottle then and went with him, followed him down a long tunnel.

Only, the memory changed, and it wasn't Huzzaq she was following anymore. It was the tiger. She sat atop the sandstone pillars of Wadi Rum in the night and bathed in streams of starlight. The shadows didn't touch her here, but the tiger slipped into the cracks. Wait here till dawn, he reminded her.

Fuck that, Noor thought coming back to the present, and went to find Yasmin.

Khayal

The old woman was finishing a can of soup in the next room.

"Where does the tunnel go?" Noor demanded.

"Which tunnel?" Yasmin answered with her own question.

Noor started to ask for the one that would lead her out of there, but then she concentrated. In her first dream about Huzzaq, she had thought he was gnarled like an olive tree. Taking a chance that it might mean something to Yasmin, she responded, "To the olive grove."

Yasmin was shocked. "Did he tell you about the grove?"

"Only in a manner of speaking," Noor said.

"It's near Madaba," Yasmin told her reluctantly, "but Noor, you cannot go there. Your uncle thinks you are dead. You mustn't leave."

"If he truly thinks I'm dead, he'll have no reason to free Nur, or Huzzaq for that matter. His only use for Nur now is to lure me out. And that's exactly what he'll do to ensure I am dead."

"We can't go!" Yasmin fought her.

"Don't you see? I have to. Now. If Nur thinks I am dead, there's no telling what he'll do, and I won't have the same stain on his soul as mine. Now show me the way."

Chapter 22: Spark

While, in theory, a man might be better able to guess what another man might do than a woman would, this man was her uncle. And the other man, well, whatever he was, he was hers. Noor was good at her job for a reason. She needed to get there fast. It would never be on her turf- she had no place- but she wouldn't be chased again. She'd meet this head on.

Yasmin showed Noor downstairs to the tunnels. Noor was surprised to see electric mine cars. She wondered if they still worked, when Yasmin flipped up an enormous generator lever and 220 volts hummed to life along the rails. Looking over the car, she saw it was operated by one simple lever; she assumed you pushed it forward to go and back to brake. There would be no turning around.

"Are you sure this is the right car?" Noor asked.

"Yes. You'll take this for about twenty minutes until the track stops. When it does, get out and move to your left. You'll find a door and through it, there will be a truck waiting for you."

"Aren't you coming?"

"No, I'll go back up to call for help and make sure to get you a car at the end. From there, take the Desert Highway to Madaba. It should take four hours, but I'll arrange for a guide. No doubt you'll get there faster."

"What am I in for?"

"I have no idea. I haven't been there in 30 years," she said. She kissed both of Noor's cheeks then. *"Ma'assalama* (Go in peace)." Noor almost laughed aloud.

Well, this is terrifying, Noor thought. She climbed into the small metal bucket of a miner's car, feeling the electricity surging through the metal. At least it made her feel alive. *For the moment.*

There were no lights and, once in the car, Noor switched off the flashlight. No sense in wasting the batteries and there was no need to steer. She took a breath and disengaged the emergency brake. She wrapped a sweaty palm around the lever and slowly pressed it forward. The cart pitched forward faster than she expected. She took a minute to acclimate to the feel of it and then gradually pushed the lever as far forward as it would go. There was nothing to do except ride.

There was no real dampness here like one might imagine in a cave or tunnel. She smelled old industrial grease, the acrid burnt stench of electricity, like insects lured into a bug zapper. There was old dust- part sand, part man and part bat guano. She flicked the flashlight on for a moment and then decided it was much better if she couldn't see the metal rails suspended beneath her. She jerked around a corner but maintained her seat. She tried to determine how much time had passed. Seven, eight minutes? *Okay, almost half way there,* she comforted herself. She was nauseated. Best she could tell, she was moving about 40 kilometers an hour, fast enough for her hair to stream back in the wind created by the movement.

Without a visual point upon which to fix her gaze, she was quickly growing dizzier and more nauseated. She slowed her breathing, concentrating on the noise. There was still the hum and occasional spark of electricity. The wind blew like a faint whistle in the chamber, but she could tell each time a section of track had been connected because there was a different "che`che`che`che" sound and an almost imperceptible bump each time it connected. It seemed close to 20 minutes. She was afraid the track would just end, and she'd crash if she didn't slow down.

Just before she clicked on the flashlight, a sliver of light appeared ahead. It must be the door, she reckoned, and immediately pulled the brake back has hard as she could, coming to a screeching halt. Once stopped, she flicked on the flashlight and thanked God she hadn't seen what was in front of her- rock. She had stopped just a meter shy of the end of the track.

"Noor?" she heard a voice call out.

"Here, Jiddo."

And his flashlight's beam met hers as he came towards her.

"Let's go," he said, putting an arm around her.

Outside the entrance was a government fueling center. Jiddo hopped into one of the white Mercedes trucks clearly marked as a government Water and Waste vehicle. She eyed him suspiciously but said nothing. He reversed and then dropped into second gear until they climbed out of the sand and back onto the highway. The dashboard clock read 2:43am.

Jiddo followed her gaze. "Sunrise is in four hours. We must hurry."

She supposed her uncle would have the benefit of familiar terrain, but still, she wanted to be there before dawn and have a chance to get the lay of the land. Jiddo stepped on the gas, inching up the red needle on the speedometer. When it neared 160kph, the truck began to shake, but the older man did not.

"We'll get there in two and a half hours if we don't slow down until we near the city."

Noor nodded.

Chapter 23: In the Grove

Nur felt the change coming. If it was atmospheric or spiritual or just a gradual lessening of the darkness, he couldn't say. A man had come into the room where they were keeping him. He told Nur that he was free to leave. Nur made a derisive sound indicating disbelief. The man said, "She's dead. Kadir has no more use for you."

He followed the man down a series of corridors. At the end of one, the man opened the door to the pre-dawn sky and roughly shoved Nur out and locked the door. He had no idea where he was.

Nur heard the words, yet he didn't seem able to process them. *Think,* he commanded himself. He felt sure that if she were really dead, he'd know it somehow, feel it in his bones. *Okay,* he thought, *either she is dead, or Kadir thinks she is. If he believes her dead, what motivation does he have to let me go? What use am I to him?* He could see no point in her uncle leaving him alive. *Unless,* Nur reasoned rather quickly, *Kadir suspects that she isn't dead and wants to use me to lure her out.* That made the most sense. But first, he had to get a handle on where he was.

The dawn had not yet emblazoned its riotous russet red streaks on the horizon, but the sky was already a lighter shade of charcoal grey. Once his eyes began to adjust, or his eye rather, as the other was swollen shut where he'd been punched, he could see the outlines of rows of trees. Only one kind of tree had such gnarled trunks and canopy tops-olive trees. They were overgrown at this part, but he could make out the careful rows in the near distance. Olives, for the most part, are only farmed in the northwest corner of the country, north of the Dead Sea. He'd need to move east and south to get to Aqaba, but if he were at the southern tip of the fertile valley, it'd be some time until he came upon a town. *North, then*, he thought. But the stars were already fading, and he had no way of knowing which way was north. So he guessed, and hoped he was right. He started to walk in his chosen direction, waiting for the sun to come up so he could confirm it.

A more unsettling possibility occurred to him then. *What if Noor wanted him to believe she was dead? What if she only wanted to disappear, and he was but a casualty? What if*, and he was surprised this had never occurred to him while he was imprisoned, *she was in on this from the beginning and had conspired to have him kidnapped? What if she were helping her uncle get rid of the rug shop and all it stood for? She didn't know they were going to Al Karak until that morning, but he supposed they could have called her, too. No*, he told himself and then more firmly, *no. She wouldn't. But she said so herself- he didn't know what she was capable of.* Distracted in the dark, he tripped over a rock and rolled down a ravine, coming to a halt only when his head stopped him by smacking into a small boulder, rendering him unconscious.

Jiddo brought the truck to a stop off the side of road, driving slowly with just the parking lights on, until he found a spot where the truck would be invisible from the road. He tossed a backpack to Noor and told her she'd find what she needed in it. He got out and moved to the truck bed and started checking ammo.

Noor opened the bag and found her black cargo pants, black boots, black tank top and black long sleeved button up. She smiled. Now, at least she could feel like herself, like she was prepared for the job at hand. She shimmied into the pants and tank in the cab of the truck and put on the rest after she opened the door. Noor made her way to the bed of the truck to meet Jiddo.

He dug through the duffel, handing her items one at a time, starting with a headlamp. He had a flak vest and a separate MOLLE (Modular Lightweight Load-carrying Equipment) tactical medic kit. Noor put on the head flashlight and vest, and began checking the pockets. Jiddo had put mostly 9mmmagazines in, but he hadn't yet handed her a gun. Noor flipped open the tactical kit. Inside was the PPE (Personal Protection Equipment)- she tossed out everything but the gloves. She next opened the PAT (Patient Assessment Tools) and threw out all of it- stethoscope, thermometer, oximeter. From the Trauma Supplies, she kept the Gecko grip tape, Bolin chest seals, SWAT-T tourniquets, scissors, bandages, packs of Celox hemostatic dressing, Israeli bandages, collapsible bag valve, endotracheal intubation and King Tubes.

By this time, Jiddo had laid out an assortment of guns on the tailgate of the truck. Noor picked up two Heckler & Koch VP9s and checked them before storing one in her thigh belt and the other in her vest. She picked up the MP5 submachine gun. The MP7 had a hell of a lot more stopping power, but the MP5 took the same 9mm ammo as the pistols, saving her valuable carry room. She was going in light. And though she would shoot to kill if she had to, like she was trained to do, she didn't want to anymore if she could help it.

Noor nodded to the pistol Jiddo strapped on his hip. "Had that awhile?" She smiled at him. The guns had very few changes over the years, but the hilt was worn smoother around his grip.

Jiddo reverently picked up the Colt 1911 .45, with the mid-60s brown hilt on the otherwise flat black weapon. "My service weapon." he said as he loaded the magazine. "It's never failed me."

She picked up the MP5, dropped the magazine out to double check that it was fully loaded, slid it back in and tugged to make sure the magazine was secure. She slid the shoulder strap over her right shoulder and over her neck. She filled her left cargo pockets with extra magazines. Jiddo had done the same, in addition to the holster he carried around his waist, but on his left side. He held up a night vision device (NVD) and a THERM-APP. The NVD was second generation, but it had a pretty decent infrared illuminator mounted to help amplify the light. She'd never seen this kind of thermal camera device before. Jiddo had two Android phones with cameras. He attached a small device about the size of a cell phone battery over each camera and plugged it into the phone. He grinned and held it up for her to look.

"Holy shit!" she whispered, staring wide-eyed at Jiddo.

It was amazing. The THERM-APP turned a phone into a thermal monocular. It was sensing the heat coming off Jiddo and applying colors to the different degrees, forming a kind of pixilated picture. The focus was awful, which is why they still needed the NVD, but where there was no contrast or not enough light, the THERM-APP would be a huge help in addition to the NVDs. She'd be able to pick up the heat signature of even a mouse.

The last thing he offered her was ear protection- the good ones that amplify quiet sounds while still reducing other ranges. Jiddo tossed the rest of the ammunition and two liter bottles of water into the daypack and everything else back into the duffel.

Jiddo nodded and moved to take his place, slightly ahead of her, at her left.

She could barely think on the drive, but now thoughts raced through her head. *What if Nur was still inside? What if he wasn't, but she didn't know it and had to go in and check? Where the hell was Huzzaq?* She missed the old bastard now. How many times had it been his voice she heard in her earpiece, directing her, on one of these missions? She wished she had him now.

Focus. On the ride, Jiddo had explained there were numerous underground tunnels around the house in the olive grove. They'd either look like ruins or be completely hidden. Each one connected back to another and to the main house, which had a safe room underground. The last time Jiddo was here 30 years ago, the back tunnel off the courtyard was collapsed, as was the northwest facing one from the left side of the house. Unless Kadir knew they were coming, he'd be in the main house, but it was too well guarded to approach directly. Jiddo would take the lead clearing and, being left-handed, would cover her left side.

"You tap me when you're ready to move. If I need to reload, I'll say 'red' and then 'green' when reloaded. And nod when the area is clear."

Every team had a similar version of these instructions.

"Don't speak unless you have to," he added.

Jiddo turned her around and checked that the four flash-bangs strapped to her vest between her shoulder blades were secure.

"Talking isn't going to matter if we have to use these." She nodded back towards the flash-bangs.

"We won't until the last minute. C'mon, let's go."

Chapter 24: The Fatal Funnel

Noor didn't care much for taking second. Most of her missions were solo, and on the rare occasion she'd had a partner, she had insisted on being lead. It was the more dangerous role, always open to a hit for a second or two before a partner, but she could control the pace and didn't have to wait until the other decided to move. But Nur was Jiddo's grandson. And who was Nur to her? She didn't know exactly, but she felt a piercing sense of possession, so much so that she felt her connection to him trumped family. Surely that meant something. But now wasn't the time.

They had moved in a wide arc, starting inside the craggy berm on the north side, and circling about 315 degrees-almost a full circle around the property- staying behind cover of the olive trees. They'd have to approach the house if Jiddo couldn't find a tunnel, but there would be cameras, guards and likely tripwire to navigate.

Just then, Jiddo put up his hand and signaled for her to stop and wait. He moved forward, while she covered him, slicing the 90 degrees around him, scanning for movement. He disappeared behind some thick scrub for a moment, and then moved back towards her.

"The tunnel door is open."

"A trap?" she asked.

"Could be, but I don't think they have any clue we could be here yet."

Huzzaq. She didn't say so, but she felt sure Huzzaq was here already and had unlocked the tunnel. He had said not to come, but even if he thought she'd obey, he'd still want to leave the exits open for himself. If he made it out. If any of them did…

The sun was just coming up over the horizon, but it was already lighting up the sky, limning the trees in a backlit rose gold. She took a minute to reorient herself before moving. The sun was coming up behind the tunnel entrance, so the tunnel faced west. If she came back out this tunnel, the truck would be in the northwest corner of the grove.

"Noor, the tunnels should be safe enough. If they're not expecting an attack, they'll all be in the house. But go slow, let's clear everything first. When we get to the house, we'll see if the entrance is also unlocked, or blow it open. Ready?" Noor nodded.

At the scrubline, Jiddo got down and crawled through the spinichristi shrubs. Noor got down and followed. In the middle of the patch of spinichristi was a slightly sloped bifold metal shelter door. The rusted chain that had secured it was tossed to the side. Jiddo looked to Noor and upon her nod, she pulled back the right door, taking cover underneath it momentarily, while Jiddo pulled the left open and swung himself in, scanning the area. He nodded to Noor, who dropped the door the rest of the way down and made to follow him.

There was a steel ladder secured to the wall, running about six meters down before the tunnel opened and moved parallel with the earth above.

150

"There's no cover here. Wait till I get down. If it's clear, I'll flash the light three times," Jiddo said.

Jiddo kept three points on the ladder at all times as he climbed in the dark. Noor thought she'd go mad for the waiting. He was actually moving pretty quickly, even for someone half his age. At the base, Jiddo jumped the last few feet and pulled the THERM-APP out of his pocket to view down the tunnel. He flashed a light up at her three times. She rotated the strap on the MP5 to her back, scaled the ladder, and joined Jiddo at the bottom a minute later. The tunnel was made of interlocking concrete sections, like drain pipes, with reinforced rebar fittings. And aside from the dust, crickets and spiders, it was fairly clean- not much evidence of rats or scorpions, but no evidence of anything else either. She didn't think Huzzaq, or anyone else, had come this way in quite some time.

Jiddo moved against the left side of the tunnel, and Noor stayed close to the right to avoid the fatal funnel in the middle. A few meters ahead, a second tunnel intersected to the right. Jiddo held his hand to stop her and crossed to the right side ahead of Noor. He counted down on his fingers, and on "one," he dropped to a low crouch and quickly made his way to the other side of the opening. He nodded and they both crept slowly into the tunnel, careful to expose as little of their bodies as possible, as she cleared the left and he cleared the right side of the tunnel. Satisfied that the immediate portion of the tunnel was clear, she looked to him for direction. He chose to head back to the first section, reckoning it was the most direct path to the house.

And it would have been the most direct path had the tunnel not been blocked at the end. It had been intentionally walled up with cinder blocks- *maybe to make a storeroom,* she thought. They backtracked to the intersecting tunnel, and this time went left. It's hard to tell how long a dark tunnel is, but Noor thought they had been going about 100 meters when they saw another intersection up ahead. They used a similar clearing technique for the T-intersection. Though she trusted her night-vision goggles to some extent, she used the THERM-APP, too. Other than the pale pinprick images of insects and mice, there was no one.

Jiddo was sure the house lay to the left, but all the same, he wanted to follow the tunnel all the way to the right. He wanted to make sure if they needed to come back this way, they could actually get out. As much as he'd prefer to be certain they weren't followed, that threat existed anyway with whoever had the keys, or the ability to force the door open.

So Noor moved just to the left, and as Jiddo went right, she did her best to cover him while checking both directions periodically for thermal activity. After what seemed like a long time, Jiddo flashed his light three times and started back towards her.

"The door is unlocked," he whispered to her, "same as the other. Someone's unchained the doors, but not come down."

She was sure it was Huzzaq. Either he unlocked the doors for himself in case he needed to make a quick exit, or he knew she would follow him. The question was, did he get inside already or was he still out here somewhere? What if Kadir had already killed him? Worse, what if she ran into him in the tunnels and shot him? There was nothing she could do but rely on her instincts.

They proceeded to the left side of the tunnel and followed it to its end. Noor had prepared for the need to open steel doors, but like at the outset, they were mysteriously left unlocked, too. Noor was beginning to wonder if they had a friend on the inside helping Huzzaq, or if he had done all this himself.

Chapter 25: Breach

Jiddo took the lead into the basement bunker under the house. The three doors connected to this room were all unlocked and left slightly ajar. They followed the wide trail of displaced dust on the floor over to the only staircase. A body was slumped under the staircase. Noor forced herself to look. It was the man she met at Al Karak, the man who came to bargain with her- Huzzaq's life for Nur's. Out of habit, she checked to make sure Jiddo was covering her, and bent to take the man's pulse. She hadn't seen any blood, no obvious head wounds or a concussion. No pulse. She reached behind his neck to check for a break, and instead found a syringe sticking out. *Succinylcholine*, she thought immediately, and the look of open-eyed paralysis on the man's face confirmed it for her. *Where the hell would he have gotten that?*

Noor rose in disgust and motioned to Jiddo to start up the stairs. They needed to get in the house and get this- whatever it was- done, and fast. At the top of the stairs, they took care breaching the entry. It was quiet- too quiet. Noor kept her hands glued to the MP5. They found two bodies in two separate rooms. Both men were sitting in chairs with no pulse and syringes in their necks. Rather than being comforted by three fewer guards to contend with, Noor's alarm actually rose. A stranger couldn't just sneak up on them and kill them; they trusted whoever did this, and she very much doubted that that person was Huzzaq.

The downstairs was clear, so they made their way upstairs to the bedrooms on the east side of the house. In the third bedroom, they found Huzzaq bleeding, gagged and bound to a bed. In her panic, she ran to him before Jiddo could stop her. Kadir, seemingly from nowhere, came in and shot at Jiddo's back. She spun around and found her uncle holding a .45 trained at her.

"Untie him and take the gag off," he said to Noor.

"What?" Noor asked, but did as she was told.

Huzzaq got up.

"Take her guns," Kadir commanded Huzzaq.

He did. She stared incredulously at Huzzaq. He wouldn't make eye contact with her.

"Finish him," he said to Huzzaq, motioning to the rocking form of Jiddo, who was bleeding on the floor in the doorway.

"First, tell me where she is," Huzzaq demanded.

"Where who is?" Noor interjected.

"Yasi! Your uncle took her!"

"Kill him first," Kadir said, devoid of any emotion.

Huzzaq fired two more shots into the downed Jiddo. Kadir laughed mercilessly.

"You fool!" Noor screamed at Huzzaq. "Yasi is fine! He doesn't have her!"

Noor made to charge at Huzzaq in a rage, not caring at all that her uncle still had a gun trained on her.

Huzzaq was undecided. He didn't know whether he should believe Noor or Kadir. He had always wanted Yasmin. He'd do anything to have her. He looked down at the form of his friend on the ground, and knew he had failed. A life of distrust and violence had caught up with him. In that moment of recognition, of weakness, Kadir turned and fired at Huzzaq.

The .45 caliber bullet exited the right side of his head in a spray of blood and brains onto the hallway wall. For a split second, she saw the surreal beauty in the arching red rainbow shape his life left behind.. The sun shone through the east-facing windows, casting everything in red and gold hues. She turned to face her uncle.

"Well, I could use a drink," he said, as though nothing had happened. "Shall we?"

When she didn't move, he spun her around, gun firmly pressed under her shoulder blade. "Let's go downstairs."

Noor had to stretch long across Jiddo's body to breach the door. She walked downstairs and into the living room as her uncle directed her.

"Pour me a drink," he said.

Noor uncorked the bottle of whiskey and poured it, straight, into a highball glass on the bar.

Kadir laughed. "Remember the last time you made me a drink, Khayal?" He nearly coughed her name, with the rough Arabic guttural "kh" sound.

"How could I forget?"

His smile was more of a sneer.

"When I agreed to take you in, I had no idea how much trouble you would be," he said, feigning lightheartedness. "I should have had them rape you so you would know your place and who had the power."

"And I should have made sure you were dead, Uncle," she returned levelly.

He chuckled at her. "Ah, my tempest, let's talk, for old time's sake." And he settled into a wing chair, drink in one hand, the gun in the other, resting leveled at her.

"I don't feel much like chatting."

He purposefully shot just to her left, shattering a bottle on the bar. "Pity, as the only use you have to me now is information." She couldn't mistake the message- he was a man of action, even if he wanted to talk right now.

"What do you want to know?"

"How long was Huzzaq working to undermine me?"

"I don't know, Uncle, why don't you ask him? Oh, yes, that's right. You killed him already."

"What do you care? He killed your man upstairs. It was his plan to take Nur."

Noor considered this for a moment. It could be true. It may not. "I don't care, Uncle. In fact you saved me the trouble, so thank you." That may have also been a half-truth.

"Ah, Khayal, if only you were more obedient, we could have made a wonderful team!" He smiled almost fondly, almost paternally at her.

"What of the other men here? Did you kill them, too?" she asked.

"They were compromised."

"Compromised? How so?"

"I couldn't be sure they weren't loyal to Huzzaq, and even if not, I couldn't have them see that one of my own could turn against me. So either way, they had to go."

"I assume you used Succinylcholine? How did you get it?" Noor asked. She was both painfully aware she needed to end this, yet for the moment, keeping him talking was the only thing keeping her alive.

He clapped. "So smart! How I wish you had followed in my footsteps! I bought a drug company in Canada. They manufactured the drug for use in lethal injections, but then all those American liberals stopped most of the executions. When the Canadians realized the US wasn't just using the drug for anesthesia, they quit selling it to them. So you see,

I have more than I can sell. But not necessarily more than I can use!" He laughed again.

"Clever," she said sarcastically.

"Yes, yes it was, wasn't it?" he said, unfazed.

"So, as entertaining as this is, what do you plan to do with me? Bury me here? Where are we, anyway?"

The most rueful smile she had ever seen from him crossed his face then. "You really don't remember, do you?" he laughed. "It's funny, of course, but even I am not without feeling. It's sad too, *Noor.*"

"What's sad, Uncle? That you killed my parents? And hundreds of others? That you tortured and abused me?"

"Oh, my little black cloud," he said, leaning forward to touch her face, "this was your parents' home," and he leaned back to watch the impact of his words contort her face. "I've brought you home to die!" He laughed, but only for a moment.

Chapter 26: Pleural Space

Nur awoke just after dawn, with the sun blaring into his face. He opened his eyes but still could see nothing. One eye was completely swollen shut. He took the inside of his t-shirt and attempted to wipe his other eye clear of the crusted blood that had resealed it. It hurt like hell, but he had to see to move. He tried to remember what had awoken him when he heard the rapport of gunfire. And like air through a crack, he moved toward it.

Noor lunged at Kadir. She no longer cared that he had a gun sighted on her, or that she was without a weapon. She herself *was* a weapon. He had used her that way for so long, and now she would use it against him. She jumped and kicked the gun from his hand, where it went spinning across the floor. She was like an animal, going straight for the face, the jugular, wherever her fingers could find purchase. He backhanded her across the face, and rolled on top of her to try to keep her arms pinned down. But she spun again and kneed him hard in the groin. She should have used this moment to run, but she couldn't. This had to end. He had to end.

Noor reached for any object within reach, smacking him in the head with the bottle of whiskey nearby. It stunned him for a moment, but he went right back to attacking her with renewed gusto. Sitting on her chest, his knees pinning Noor's arms, Kadir banged her head into the floor and then placed his hands, rough with black curly hair , around her neck and began to squeeze the life out of her.

In contrast to the mad stramash between them, the room was quiet as he choked her. The silence allowed the click of a pistol being cocked to echo throughout the room. Before Kadir could turn around, Nur shot him through the back. He collapsed onto Noor, but instantly loosened his grip around her throat. She turned her head away from the body on top of her, struggling to replace the air in her lungs.

Nur ran to her, set the gun down, and hauled Kadir's motionless body off of Noor. He helped her to her feet, beginning a sigh of relief, when he felt the pistol muzzle push into his own back. Kadir laughed a joyless laugh.

"Come to save your girlfriend?" he chuckled.

Seeing the gun to Nur's back, she felt her chest constrict even more than when she was being choked.

"NOOOOOOOO!" she screamed, shoving Nur away, as five shots resounded through the small room.

Jiddo had used what lifeblood was still in him to drag himself, slowly and silently, down the stairs. At the base, he used the handrail for leverage to pull himself into an upright position. He took in the scene quickly. He could avoid Noor, but in shooting at Kadir, he could easily hit

Nur. With the deep breath of a prayer, he unleashed five shots at Kadir, and promptly collapsed onto the stairs.

Noor wasn't sure if the scream came from Nur or Kadir. She felt bad about it, but went first to her uncle, taking his pulse to determine that he was, in fact, dead. That ascertained, she gently rolled Nur over from his supine position. One side of his face was swollen and blooming purple with bruises. Blood poured out of his chest. She grabbed her MOLLE, stopping to check Jiddo on the way back. She didn't see how could be alive at all, with at least three shots in him from upstairs. He waived her away. "Save the boy," he said.

Noor opened her medical tactical bag and ripped open the outer layer packaging of the Israeli bandage. She opened the Chitosan and applied it to the wound, just above his heart. She reached under to feel if the bullet had exited or stayed in the body. She felt the marble sized hole under his shoulder blade.

"Fuck," she muttered.

"I thought you were trying not to curse," Nur feebly joked.

"I AM trying, wise-ass! Don't speak," she hissed at him. "Do you think you can sit up for a moment?"

"Yes," he whispered, laboring to an upright position with her assistance. "Why are you asking me questions if you want me to be quiet?"

She rolled her eyes and placed a second pack of Chitosan on the exit wound. She made sure she could still get to his upper ribs, and unwound the Israeli bandage around his ribcage. Once she made the first round, she ran the bandage back through the plastic loop and reversed direction. This clip worked just like a belt buckle and kept tension on the site without having to apply a lot of force. She completely unrolled and wrapped the rest, securing it with the end clip, pausing for a moment to make sure the blood loss was slowing.

But his pulse was high, his breathing was rapid and shallow, his trachea appeared to have moved to the opposite side of his neck and he was taking on that faintly blue color people do when hypoxic. She placed her head on his chest, listening for a telltale whistling or sucking sound.

"Goddamn it," she said.

"What is it?" he whispered.

"Didn't I tell you not to talk? Your blood isn't oxygenating enough," she replied.
"You have a tension pneumothorax."

"What's-?" he asked but stopped when she glared at him.

"Air buildup in the pleural space. The gunshot lacerated your lung, which is allowing air to leak out, but obstructs venous return to the heart." Seeing his look of confusion, she added, "It's a partial lung collapse that prevents the blood from getting enough oxygen back to the heart. I'm going to have to fix it."

"How?"

"Stop talking or I'll tape your mouth shut," she said tersely.

She drew a syringe of 10mg of morphine and injected it in his arm. He'd need more, she knew, but was afraid to suppress his breathing more until the pneumothorax was under control. Noor reached for the package of iodine and wiped it across his chest. The blue tint to his skin was worse, but he'd noticeably calmed from the morphine and the pain seemed to have diminished somewhat. She needed to do the thoracostomy *now*.

She found the space under the fourth rib in the mid-clavicular line and in a quick stabbing motion, punctured his lung with a 14-gauge cannula. The instantaneous expulsion of air out of the catheter confirmed her diagnosis.

He was breathing better now, and the bluish tinge was starting to recede. He had fallen asleep, or passed out from the pain and shock. That was okay though. She needed to think, and to check on Jiddo.

Making her way over to the older man, she felt sure he would be alive, though she had no real reason to believe he would be. Noor knelt, taking his hand in hers. She took his pulse and could see the shallow but steady movement of his chest. He couldn't stay crumpled on the stairs like that, but she didn't want to move him until she checked the extent of damage he'd taken.

Noor unbuttoned his shirt, taking in the two divots in the Kevlar vest where Huzzaq had shot him. At close range, the side-by-side bullets had penetrated the vest, but not by much. She unstrapped the vest from his sides and eased it over his head. Both of Huzzaq's bullets had penetrated the right side of his chest, but were partially exposed on the surface. She applied an occlusive dressing to the site. His arm was another matter. Most of the blood came from his inner left arm about two inches above his elbow, where Kadir had shot him. The blood spattered onto his chest, making the chest shots appear more damaging. She estimated that about twenty minutes had passed since the shot. She contemplated using the tourniquet, but the blood had already slowed, so she decided to start with the Chitosan and pressure bandage, rather than risk losing his arm.

Jiddo was trying to talk now, but she couldn't tell if he had said Nur or Noor.

"He's okay. I'm okay," she assured him.

"Tell Yasi I'm sorry. I tried, but I couldn't save him."

"You did save him! Nur is going to be ok."

"No. Huzzaq." He promptly fell unconscious again.

Noor had about a minute to contemplate Jiddo's message and what the hell she was going to do next, when the tinny whining of sirens broke the silence.

With the head trauma and stress, the sirens threatened to explode the raging migraine in her brain. But she did as she was trained. When the police shouted at the door, she gave them a brief accounting, saying that all assailants were dead, two other casualties severely wounded, plus herself, all unarmed. The police swept in and cleared the rooms one by one anyway, radioing back to the medics to call a second ambulance, and another vehicle to take away the dead.

Once the rooms were clear and EMTs came in, she gave them the status on Jiddo and Nur.

"Male, late 20s, GSW- Chitosan applied, 10mg morphine administered about 20 minutes ago, tension pneumothorax caused by laceration to lung, hypoxic decrease post-thoracostomy. Male, 60, multiple GSW- two to chest superficial, third GSW in upper arm, hemostatic and occlusive dressing applied, major blood loss. I'm 27 and really banged up and could use some Toradol for this fucking migraine."

The lead EMT nodded and went to retrieve the Toradol, whispering to the policeman closest as he did so, "You've got about 60 seconds if you want to ask her anything. After this," he said, flicking an air bubble out of the syringe, "she's gonna be out like a light till tomorrow."

The cop hurried over to Noor while the EMT injected the Toradol. "Miss, what happened here?"

"Family reunion. My uncle," she nodded towards Kadir's body, "was a bad mother…" she laughed as the Toradol coursed through her veins, alleviating all feeling and attachment to reality.

Chapter 27: Tiger's Song

It was the same dream, only she and the tiger weren't running this time. He was curled into a chair, his overlarge legs overhanging the arms of the chair. That's odd, *she thought. But when she blinked, the tiger had risen and was lying next to her, softly purring. The humming transferred from his skin to hers as a faint vibration of warmth. Then she heard him sing in that same deep purr-*

> When the gibbous moon
> bloomed,
> The stars receded back,
> And all her former skins
> Were no longer stained black.

Noor awoke late the next day without the migraine but with the dull, full headache of a Toradol hangover. She expected to see rows of hospital beds in the women's wing, but instead she had her own room, with orange roses in a vase on the windowsill. A nurse came in, revealing the presence of several police officers standing outside the door, who then followed behind her, despite the nurse's protests.

"I'm sorry, Miss. They've been waiting all night. I kept them out as long as I could," the nurse said.

"It's ok. Better to get it over with…"

The lead officer stood at the foot of her bed, allowing the nurse to carry on, but not delaying his mission either. He introduced himself and his men- names which she promptly forgot- and asked her for a statement. She didn't answer for several moments. The officer grumbled and the nurse interjected with "Head trauma, you imbecile!" Perhaps she should use that excuse. How else would she explain her own part, and the weapons?

"Miss," he interrupted her thinking. "We need you to give a statement regarding the events that occurred outside of Madaba early yesterday morning. Do you understand? Do you wish for a lawyer?"

"My uncle killed his own men, shot Jiddo once and forced another man to fire two more shots into him. He tried to kill me and Nur, but Jiddo slid down the stairs and killed Kadir," she said simply.

The officer looked to the more junior of his men to make sure he was writing this down. Satisfied that he was, he turned his gaze back to Noor. "As admirably succinct as that is, Miss, I'm afraid it doesn't really tell us much, or explain why," he said gruffly.

"Well, it's a rather long story." An unknown man, about 60 years old, in full military dress spoke as he entered and closed the door.

"Sir!" The officer saluted the man. He did not know him, but from his appearance and double Arab sword insignia crossed under a crown on his uniform, he was a very high-ranking officer.

"I am *Fareeq*, Lieutenant General, Anwar Nejem of the Jordanian Special Operations Command (JSOC), 37th Royal Special Forces Brigade, 71st Counter-terrorist Battalion," the man announced to Noor.

"*Ammo* (Sir)," she nodded.

Fareeq Nejem turned back to the police officers. "Thank you for your assistance in this matter, but the *Fareeq Awal*, the full General of JSOC, has assumed command over this case," he said, handing the officer an official-looking document and adding, "You are dismissed."

The police were clearly unhappy about this change in plan and command, but could not say anything. Instead, they saluted and left the room, the nurse eagerly following after them.

"I had no idea I had friends in such high places," Noor said. "Would you like to sit?"

"No, Miss. I'll only take a moment of your time. The coroner was able to determine the cause and time of the fatalities, and each man was well known to us. In fact, we had been gathering intelligence on your uncle's activities for some time now. You will be cleared of any wrong-doing, and as this is now a classified matter, there were will be no public record of your involvement."

Noor had so many questions she couldn't decide where to start, and instead lumped them all into a baffled, "How?"

"That's another long story." He smiled kindly down at her. "But Ibrahim is in my command."

"You mean he *was*, like in the 1960s?" she asked, thoroughly confused as to how Jiddo could still be in the elite special forces of the military.

"I suppose you can say 'was' as I accepted his resignation this morning. But he's served with me since 1967."

It made a good deal of sense now that she thought on it: his physical prowess, access to weapons stocks, his insistence on removing the intruder from her apartment...

"I can see you have more questions." He smiled at the growing acceptance on her face. "But I'm not at liberty to answer them, and I've kept you long enough from your convalescence."

"But Ibrahim made it? He is alive?" she asked.

"He had four blood transfusions, but is doing well now," he answered and then turned to leave.

As his hand gripped the door handle to leave, he turned to her once more, almost as an afterthought. "I met your parents once, about 25 years ago. They were good people, Noor. They'd be proud of you."

Noor choked back tears and bit her lip to keep from crying out.

"Oh, and if you *ever* do anything like that again, it better be under my orders, or I'll shoot you myself!" He grinned at her and then pulled the door closed behind him.

Two tears escaped her watery eyes even as she laughed in relief.

Later that evening, Noor had a rather full room. Yasmin had rolled Jiddo into Noor's room in a wheelchair, with Anya hovering over Nur like a toddler who was about to fall at any moment.

"Why can't you just sit in the wheelchair like the damn doctor told you?" Anya barked at him.

"Hush, sister," he said placatingly but added, "You know you cannot win with me!"

"Both of you stop! Do you want to wake Noor?" Yasmin admonished.

"I'm awake," Noor said.

She was glad to see them all. The General had said Jiddo would recover, but it was something else entirely to see it with her own eyes. He looked good. Nur did too. Actually Nur looked really good, she smiled to herself.

"You saved us!" Jiddo said, holding her hand.

"No, you both saved me. And had I not gotten you into this mess, you wouldn't have needed saving! I'm so sorry. And I'm sorry about Huzzaq," she said to Yasmin.

Yasmin's hand had rested on Jiddo's shoulder, and when he moved to lay his hand on hers at the mention of Huzzaq, it did not go unnoticed by Noor. She caught Nur's eye- he had seen it too, but smiled and shrugged.

"Where's Mohammed?" Noor asked.

"At home, preparing for your return. He was quite beside himself when he thought he might lose you," Anya answered.

"Well, get some rest tonight. The doctors tell me you will all be released tomorrow, *Allah* (God), help me!" Yasmin said as she and Anya wheeled Jiddo back to his room.

"I'm so sorry," Noor said when it was just her and Nur left in the room.

"Don't be," Nur replied, slowly laying himself down on his good shoulder on her bed with a wince.

"'Don't be' he says with a gunshot wound to the chest," she said, rolling her teary eyes, attempting to wipe them away with a joke.

"We're even. We saved each other," Nur said, kissing her head.

Khayal

She felt at peace then, with the warmth of his body next to hers. And then Nur began to sing the next verse of the tiger's song-

> On the rock's precipice,
> The liliest white light,
> Grew into her soul's niche
> And erased the day's night.

And she knew, then, what she had begun to suspect months ago.

Chapter 28: Many are the Roads that Do Not Lead to the Heart- Arab Proverb

For several days, Noor made a great show of properly convalescing in her old apartment, but the truth was she was listless. If she missed a meal at the house, Yasmin came with soups and teas, and tinctures guaranteed to improve her spirit and disposition. Noor accepted them, only mildly curious as to what Yasmin was giving her. Nur and Jiddo stayed at Yasmin's. She saw them during meals, and though Jiddo would take a little longer to heal, he seemed oddly content with Yasmin's administrations. Nur, on the other hand, was also restless.

Mohammed came to her apartment on missions from Yasmin to spy on her. He checked the water heater, replaced the sink drains, changed the lock on the door, always lingering longer than necessary. The fourth time, she simply asked him to bring a backgammon board and play with her. She let him win, hoping he would open up to say whatever it was he wanted to say.

"What will you do now?" he finally asked, halfway through the second game.

"What do you mean?" she asked him.

"Will you stay in Aqaba? Or in Jordan at all?"

She wanted to reassure him somehow, but she had no answers and wouldn't lie to him.

177

"I don't know. But I do know, wherever I go, when I am settled, you can come and visit me."

He beamed at her, and her once-hardened heart softened a little bit more. She wondered why he was so attached to her, not more so than to Yasmin or Anya, but in a different way. She had the distinct feeling he looked to her as the mother he wanted. No one had ever depended on her before, not for love anyway.

Later that night, after Mohammed had grown sleepy and went home, Noor lay awake in her single bed trying to plan her next move. Again, she missed Huzzaq's voice in her ear, telling her what she must do, but now his memory was so tinged with bitterness and confusion that she pushed that aside before she became mired in it. A knock sounded at the back door.

She slipped her Heckler and Koch 9mm from under the bed and cocked it, slowly walking to the back door, while avoiding the glass portion where she could be seen. She stood by the side of the door and asked who was there.

"Nur," he whispered.

She relaxed her gun hand and opened the door to him. He took one look at her and the gun and shook his head.

"Give me that," he demanded, and for lack of anything better to do, she did.

Nur dropped the magazine out and pocketed the bullets before replacing it and setting the gun down on the counter. "Didn't the third highest-ranking military officer in all of Jordan threaten to shoot you himself if you were involved in any other gunfights?" he asked her, attempting levity but letting her know this had to stop.

"I believe so, but until his boss or the King himself tells me-" Nur silenced her sarcastic retort with a kiss.

"Stop hiding from me, Noor," he said a minute later.

"I'm not hiding. I'm... you know, figuring out what to do next."

"Shall I tell you?" He smiled at her.

"You have a suggestion?" she asked.

"Call it a request."

"I'm listening."

"Good. Throw a few changes of clothes in a bag, and let's get out of here."

"You can't be serious. Nur, you have to change your dressings and go for a follow-up visit, and..." But her heart wasn't really up to fighting him. She was as eager as he was.

"Good thing my girlfriend is a medic! Grab your MOLLE, too and you can help me with the bandages."

She quickly got her stuff together. On one knee, kneeling over her bag, she placed her clothes and toiletries in the bag and asked, "Did you call me your girlfriend?"

"Would you prefer I call you something else?" he asked, clearly teasing her. "How about 'sweetie *habibti*' (darling) or 'sexy storm' or 'quick-draw?'" He nodded to the gun on the counter.

"Ha-ha," she said drily.

"Well, I only have one more idea, then." He paused, waiting for her to look up at him. "How about 'wife?'"

She choked for a second, but always quick on her feet, she quipped, "Normally, the man is the one on one knee when he asks that."

It was probably only 30 seconds, but it seemed like an eternity hung between them then. She wouldn't accept a casual proposal, wasn't even sure it was a proposal at all. The pregnant silence swung.

"I'll keep that in mind," he finally said with a grin.

"Ugh," she sighed at him, picking up her bag and heading toward the door.

"And Noor?"

"Yeah?" She turned back to him, expectant of something.

"Can you drive? I can't manage stick yet with my right arm in a sling."

She held out her hand, like a defiant teenager, for the keys. "Anything else?"

"One last thing." He closed the distance between them and kissed her again. "*When* I ask you to marry me, you'll know without a doubt that's what I'm asking."

She fought her urge to hide behind sarcasm, and just nodded, letting another piece fall back into her heart.

Chapter 29: Inside Job

They climbed into his Range Rover around midnight. Noor adjusted the seat for her small legs and flipped through the CDs he had above the visor, selecting one to play.

"This has got to be one of the last 4-speed transmissions ever made!" she said.

They drove out of the city and onto the Dead Sea Highway. She didn't say much at first. She had been quiet ever since that awful day a week ago. *Had it only been a week? Perhaps he expected too much of her, then*, Nur thought. The silence burned like a cigarette between them. He'd wait until it burned itself out.

"Nur?" she asked tentatively. "Can I ask you something?"

"Of course."

"What happened that night at the Chinese restaurant?"

"When I caught you staring at me through the lacquered screen?" he teased her.

"I wasn't staring; I was spying. There's a distinction," she laughed.

"There was a woman we had been trying to help for a long time. We managed to get her papers and got her out."

"It seemed like everyone was celebrating... except you."

"It's hard to rejoice when she should have been free to begin with."

Noor glanced at him to see if he'd continue.

"What I do is illegal and it risks the safety of those I love."

"But it's the right thing to do," she countered.

"It is. So I do it. No, that's not exactly true. I do it because I can't not do it. When it gets too hard, I remind myself that it's morally right, that the ends justify the means."

Noor said, "For me, it was almost always fast, and a choice of hit, or be hit. But there were times when my soul said no to the things I had to do. I told myself these were bad men. They did bad things to bring me there. I simply sped up their fates, and it was wrong, but at least they would do less harm."

"In an ideal world, morality would be the same as legality. But here- who's to say what's wrong or right?" Nur wondered.

"I'm scared I may no longer know the difference," she said.

Her last statement hung. Without the sound of their voices, the music took precedence. She had waited for signals, but never for signs. Now she did both.

The first album was almost over. It had made its way to the 13th track, which she hoped wasn't a bad omen, but then 13 was a number of upheaval and change, not necessarily bad. And the man on the CD sang-

Khayal

> I used to try and kill love, it was the
> highest sin
> Breathing insecurity out and in…
> How I choose to feel is how I am…
> I'll not lose my faith
> It's an inside job today
> Life comes from within your heart
> and desire.

Reaching for her hand, he said, "Noor, I don't know if there's any reconciling all this darkness with light, for either of us… but I want to try."

She didn't answer, but he felt her squeeze his hand in return.

They drove a few hours north. There were millions of stars visible in the night sky, with only the car's headlights to obscure them. Noor tried not to look at them because they were so bright and seemingly close to the horizon that it affected her depth perception. With hardly a word for the last three hours, she turned to him and said she needed to rest her eyes.

Slowing to a crawl, she drove off the shoulder into the packed sand and parked. She opened the car door and stretched her legs. Nur got out too, and lit a cigarette, leaning against the hood, watching her as she twirled beneath the sky.

Inside Job

"You'll hurt your neck looking up like that," he said.

"And gunshot wounds heal faster if you don't impair your vascular system."

He put the cigarette out. "Come." He motioned to where he stood, and patted the hood.

She pushed herself up backwards and lay back on the windshield. With one working arm, it took him a few extra graceless moments, but he joined her there. She sought his hand and held it.

"Do you think they all have names? The stars, I mean," she asked.

"Perhaps, like you, they have two." He smiled.

"I'm serious."

"There are over 100 billion stars, so I rather doubt they have all been named," he said.

"Not by us, maybe. But that doesn't mean they don't have names," she said.

"Do they need names?" he asked.

"I don't know. Usually not naming something means you don't expect it to last or to survive, like a stray cat," she said. "It's impermanent."
"Are you speaking of stars or us?" he asked, turning his head to face her.

"No, not of us. You've already given that a name." She smiled at him.

"I did," he agreed, "but you have not yet."

"To give a name requires faith. First, faith that it will survive, and second, that it will come to you when called," she laughed.

"I'm not particularly obedient." He joined in her laughter.

"Neither am I," she said, "but I know if I need you, you will come."

"So you'll give me a name, then?" he asked her, clearly amused with her roundabout profession of love.

"I will," she said, obstinately as ever.

"And what is that name?" He was determined to hear her say it.

"*Zawjy* (husband)."

"*Bahibbik* (I love you)," he said.

It was a pilgrimage of whim rather than convalescence. They stopped when they felt like it and moved on any time they pleased, no matter how preposterous the hour. If there was no inn or hotel, they slept in- or on- the car. Aside from some yellowed bruising and sore ribs, Noor was almost back to normal physically. But she would not let Nur walk too far before contriving a reason to stop, move into the shade, go somewhere with less of an incline, sit on the benches and observe rather than participate.

They drove for a long time before veering off the highway at the southernmost tip, turning to circumvent Al Karak, and heading to the Dead Sea. They rented towels and spent the day in the incandescent sun of late summer. Noor would not allow Nur in the water past his waist and made sure he was out of splash distance of other swimmers. He wanted to go in, but the wound was still too raw, so he kept it under a shirt and out of the water. This had been one of Noor's first stops upon returning to Jordan, so it seemed only fitting that she should bathe in it again now.

From the Dead Sea, they made their way north to Bethabara, where John the Baptist poured water from the Jordan River across Jesus' temple. There wasn't much to see. It looked like a small quarry, only shallowly filled with muddy rain run-off. The limestone stairs lead down into the kiddie-pool of muddy water, but she made Nur stay under the well-like cover above. She wondered if John the Baptist had any idea that he was about to change the fate of the world with that bit of muddy water. There was no chariot of fire carrying Elijah to the heavens, no Lazarus rising from the dead, no Joshua to restrain the waters of the River. She wondered where all the saints, and prophets, and water, had gone?

They decided not to cross to the West Bank or into Palestine to see Nazareth, Jerusalem, Bethlehem or the Sea of Galilee. Noor had seen enough conflict and abuse to last a lifetime, but it wasn't that she was afraid to see these things. She was more worried about what she'd do if she did. Whether she liked to believe it or not, she was used to taking orders; she was a soldier without a commander or a battlefield. The temptation of the expediency of violence was still too appealing.

So they only went as far as Bethabara before turning south to Mount Nebo. The hilltop perch offered them a spectacular view of Jericho and Jerusalem. It was here that Moses glimpsed the Holy Land for the first time, but never set foot there, dying on this, the last leg of the journey. *Like Huzzaq*, she thought. He had just seen what was possible, what he had been working towards all those years ago, before he got off course. He glimpsed it, only to lose it all before he could even hold it.

"What do you think of Yasi and Jiddo?" she asked Nur. "If Jiddo had not left, would they have gotten married?" she asked.

"I don't know. Jiddo's too polite. He meant to be respectful to his friends, going off and joining the army, removing the third wheel, but I don't think Yasi saw it that way."

"Yasi thought he didn't really want her that badly because he didn't try harder to get her?" Noor surmised.

"Something like that."

"Nur, how old is Jiddo?"
"62, why?"

"And you're 29?" she asked, knowing already.

"He's not my real grandfather," Nur said.

"You look a lot alike though," Noor said.

"People and their dogs sometimes look alike, too," he replied.

"So you just pretended? Being family and the rug shop, I mean?"

"No, *habibti*, Darling. The shop is a front, but it's also real. One cannot play pirates forever. It's a legitimate business to fall back on. And Jiddo and the rest may not be of my blood, but they *are* my family." Nur explained.

"You've never asked them about your parents, or where you come from?" she asked.

"No. I come from the Hashemite Kingdom of Jordan, and that is all I want to know."

"Tell me, did Jiddo ever marry?"

"No."

"You really do look a lot like him…"

"*Khalas* (enough)," he said. "*Yalla* (let's go)."

They continued on to Hammamat Ma'in, the hot springs in Madaba. This part of Jordan was called the fertile valley, where the Jordan River brought life to what would have otherwise been desert. The hot springs, in particular, were incredible. Waterfalls more than 40 meters high plunged down over the cliff sides and into the limestone pools and basins below. With the hot springs beneath, the water stayed 40-60 degrees Celsius, and tourists and locals, and even- supposedly- King Herod bathed in these healing waters. It wasn't hard to feel like royalty stretched out in the pools. She even let Nur get most of the way in the water. They spent the night in a luxurious hotel nearby, with white tile and blue umbrellas right under one of the waterfalls, and finally slept well that night.

The next morning, even though they had never had a plan, they got ready to go to where they'd always known they were headed. It was only twenty minutes away, so they took their time, swimming again in the morning and eating a lunch under the blue umbrellas before checking out.

Noor had not been there, aside from last week, since she was a child. She didn't have directions- didn't even know what the address was- but she felt her way towards it, her internal compass guiding her home.

Instead of parking along the road, this time she used the driveway, pulling up right next to the house- like someone who belonged. Viewed in the daylight, objectively- or at least without being covered in blood- the house was beautiful, like a much-simplified Versailles. The house stood, a long rectangle with wide doors in the middle, and many long windows on each side of the door. Date palms swayed sideways, neglected, and oleander and cypress trees staked out the yard from the olive grove, with figs off in the corners.

"Do you want to go inside?" Nur asked her.

"Not yet," she answered, so instead they walked hand-in-hand into the olive grove.

Weeds had grown around the olive trunks, but, there were quite a few olives growing on the neglected trees, despite the nutrients that were stolen by the weeds.

Noor reached up to pick one and held it out to Nur. "Do you know what kind these are?"

"Green," he said, grinning.

"I used to think green and black olives came from different trees, but it's been some time since I learned the black are just ripened longer," she said.

He took the olive, just barely splitting it open with his teeth and spitting the bitterness from his mouth. He pulled the two pieces of flesh from the pit.

"It's hard to tell when they're this under-ripe, but I think they are Nabali," he said.

"How can you tell?"

"A deductive guess. The flesh is softer than Souri olives, with a smaller pit, and I think these trees were planted before the Rasie cultivar was introduced, so I'm guessing Nabali."

"How much do you know about olives?" she asked him.

"Just slightly more than the basics," he said. "Why?"

"I was just thinking, because you know so much about *exports* and all…" she teased him.

"Do you want to stay, then?"

"I haven't made it past the front door yet, but yeah, I think I do."

"So you'll make an honest man of me, even before we marry?" he joked.

"Maybe," she said. "Come on, let's go see the house."

Epilogue: Two Months Later

Late in the morning, Iras and Charmion helped her dress, rimmed her eyes with kohl and rubbed sandalwood oil into her jet-black hair. When she laid upon the floor, they said a prayer to the goddesses Hathor and Wadjet for love and protection, and began slowly rolling her up in the rug. For almost an hour, she could hardly breathe, wrapped in the animal heat and stench of wool. Appollodorus carried the rug over his shoulder, out of the palace and through the streets until he came to the carpet merchant's shop. He entered just before the shop closed for siesta, saying only 'a gift from the Queen.' *Appollodorus gently laid the rolled carpet on the floor and left, as the merchant shut and locked the shop after him. The merchant knelt before the rug and gave it a mighty shove to unfurl the heavy weave. With a squeak of surprise and undignified flailing, the Queen laid dizzily, revealed before her lover. She struggled to sit up, with the room still spinning.* 'Nay, don't get up,' *he said in a low rumble, and then the tiger was upon her, as she laughed and bared her neck.*

They say the olive tree originated in the Biblical city of Rabbath Ammon- Amman, 6,000 years ago. Sometimes Noor felt that old, but mostly she was comforted living here, in Madaba. It was a painful decision, coming home to live where her uncle had intended her to die. In the end, it made her feel closer to her parents, and the act was ultimately another of defiance- she wouldn't let her uncle take this away from her. The olive grove had long been abandoned, not really worked or paid any attention in twenty years. But olives, like Noor, like the people who had lived in the Jordanian desert and valleys for 6,000 years, survived and flourished anyway.

It was October now, and the olive harvest was upon them. Nur and Noor had started raking the trees, making slow progress, a few days before Anya, Jiddo and Yasmin had made the drive from Aqaba to Madaba to help. It was a milestone in the year, and even more so for Nur and Noor. They wrapped nets around the bases of the trees and stood on small ladders to rake the olives from their branches into the parachutes below. As soon as that tree was clear, they'd gather the net and dump its contents into larger bins on the back of a cart.

A storm was predicted to hit late that night, and they were in a frenzy to get the olives in before the rain. Wet olives would rot and spoil. Noor knew it was unlikely they'd get much from the untended trees, but she needed a decent amount to get the farm back up and running. She looked up at the sky and instead, spotted Mohammed, who had just come to live with them, waving and grinning madly from the roof of the barn. There were no clouds yet, but the wind had picked up so she couldn't hear him straight away. He pointed out into the distance.

A half dozen trucks were pulling up around the edge of the grove. Men jumped out of the open beds, and Noor's hand went immediately to her sidearm, which was no longer there. Her heart raced. Nur placed a calming hand in the small of her back.

Khayal

"Look, *habibti* (honey). See what they carry?" he asked her. Nets, rakes, buckets, tarps. She looked back to him in wonderment.

Her neighbors had come. After working all week to get their own harvests in, they had come to help her before the storm. For Noor, who was just learning to accept the help and love of family, this was too much.

Nur welcomed the newcomers and, with the help of their neighbors, raked and brought in all but one row of olives. And if it dried out quickly, there was still a chance she and Nur could get some of those, too.

Noor had worked in near silence, afraid her voice would betray too much emotion, but she nodded gratefully each time a net was emptied, as the men called loudly, joking with one another from the treetops. One of the women said that all men were monkeys, happy only rutting in the forest, hooting to each other and swinging from the trees, which set off a titter of laughter among the other women. The laughter and singular purpose united the strangers, even as the wine-purple dusk settled sleepily around them.

When it was too dark to see, they made their way in twos and threes back to their vehicles and back to their own homes.

"How will we ever thank them?" Noor wondered aloud. "I don't even know all their names!"

Nur said, "They all share the same name- *'sadik'* (friend). And if you need them, they will come when you call." He smiled at her.

"Mellon," she said, shaking her head in amusement.

"What?"

"That was the password. And, as it turns out, the secret, too!" She laughed hysterically until she cried.

The sky opened up, loosening torrential rain, plastering her clothes to her body, and rinsing the filth- and pain- from her.

"Mohammed!" Nur called jovially into the night.

"Yes?"

"Noor has lost her mind," he stated, peeking at her to gauge her reaction. "She's laughing about melons in the pouring rain. Will you ask Yasi to draw her a hot bath?"

"Oh, she's not crazy. That's just the secret password," he said, running ahead to the house.

"Am I the only one not in on this secret?" he laughed, throwing an arm over her shoulder.

As Yasmin, Jiddo, Anya and Mohammed hovered in the kitchen, snacking and prepping for the large traditional feast of *Maftoul* and *Musakhan* tomorrow, Noor sank into the overly large bathtub upstairs, holding her breath under water until her lungs demanded she come up. She did this several times, seeking the rhythm of breath, and taking comfort in how perfectly paced this involuntary thing was. She didn't even have to try.

Nur came in the bathroom, naked, with his hands behind his back. "I have something for you," he said as he climbed in the tub with her.

She was a 27-year-old woman, and it was a completely undignified reaction, but it made her giggle like a girl, which, in turn, made him laugh and then blush.

"Open it," he said, handing her a hand towel and the first box.
She pried the lid off of the top, and stared at the large pendant inside, utterly speechless.

"The stone is a tiger's eye-" he started to explain, but she knew that perfectly well. Most unusual was the ring of diamonds surrounding it, set in elaborate filigree, with a thickly cupped diamond suspended over the middle of the tiger's eye.

"Yes."

"Yes, what?"

"Yes, I will marry you," she said moving to kiss him, sloshing water all over the floor.

"You haven't even opened your other present," he laughed when they came up for air.

She opened the second box, which contained a gold band without stones, but in the same intricate filigree as the pendant.

"I wanted you to have diamonds, but I didn't think you'd like all that on your hands, getting caught on your guns and whatnot," he teased.

"It's perfect," she said, as he slipped the necklace over her head and the ring onto her finger.

"Now that we are to be married, there should be no secrets between us," he said suddenly in mock seriousness. "What the hell is this 'melon' business?"

"Tolkien. 'Speak friend and enter'. Mellon is the Elvish word for 'friend'," she explained.

Nur leaned toward her, whispered in her ear, "in that case... Mellon."

Author's Post Script

Throughout the novel, when Arabic is "spoken", it's *written* in English letters. Both the sound and meaning are translated into a totally different form of writing, which poses a great deal of variation, even beyond regional dialects and slang. I'm writing about Jordanians, in Jordan, so to the extent possible, I use the more common Jordanian translations. So, for example, where readers may be familiar with *tabouli* (which is the Lebanese spelling), I have used *tabbouleh*, which reflects the accent and spelling Noor would use.

It was important to me to use the characters' own language, but not to take the reader out of the action by having to stop and consult the appendix. I tried to make the Arabic easy to spot with italics, and easy to understand with in-text translations or context clues. The Appendix is here for reference, and, as a non-scientific creative endeavor, I editorialize as much as I like, which I hope you will also enjoy.

Feel free to tell me so (or no), or to ask me questions at:

https://www.facebook.com/AmalgamistBooks

https://www.goodreads.com/author/show/8430662.Cristel_Orrand

AmalgamistBooks@gmail.com

Cristel

Glossary

ARABIC WORDS

Agal: a black, coiled, silky rope used to secure the kaffiyeh headdress.

Al: is the definitive article ("the") in Arabic and precedes many locations and names.

Allah: God.

Allah ysalmek: goodbye, literally "go with God" to a female. "ysalmak" to a male.

Ammo: honorific title, "sir".

Ana bekhair: I'm fine (in response to "how are you?").

Awal: a full military General.

Bahibbik: I love you.

Chador: black full dress/covering. A chador may be worn with or without a veil. Women in Jordan are NOT required to wear to it. Where Khayal does wear it, it's a narrative device. At the Dead Sea, I use it almost as a cocoon she comes out of at the start of this journey. Also called hijab.

Dinar: Jordanian currency. 1 USD is about .70 JD lately.

Dishdasheh: a men's dress, with the jallabieh, or the traditional ankle length tunic.

Fareeq: Lieutenant General.

Habibi/Habibti: masculine and feminine versions of an endearment- baby, honey or darling.

Hookah: tobacco water pipe, usually quite beautiful painted glass and brass.

Kaffiyeh: the traditional red-and-white-checkered Jordanian headdress. The Palestinian and Arab headdresses are usually black and white.

Keef halak: How are you? To ask a female this question, the phrase changes to "Keef halek".

Khalas: enough, stop. The "Kh" sound in Arabic is a very strong, breathy and throat-clearing "H".

Ma-salaam: the literal translation is "go with God". It means "goodbye" and is said to the one leaving.

Marhaba: hello.

Ma'assalama: a form of "goodbye" in Arabic, which literally means "go in peace". This is funny to Noor, because she's on her way into battle.

Nakheel: date palm tree.

Nebk: "spine of Christ" or spinichristi thorn bush.

Palestine: Depending on your perspective or politics, it might be called Israel; Noor, Nur, Yasmin, Ibrahim, Anya and Mohammed would say Palestine. I've chosen their voice and perspective throughout.

Sabah el khair: good morning.

Sadik: friend.

Salam: hello.

Shukrun: thank you.

Siq: a narrow canyon, crevasse. The pathway through the canyon into Petra starts where about six people can easily walk abreast, and towards the end, just before it opens into the city, narrows to where about two people can walk.

Wadi: a valley. Wadi Rum, then, is "the valley of the moon".

Winti: and you? Usually asked after saying "I'm fine" in response to "how are you?"

Yalla: hurry, go. Used the way we might say "c'mon."

Zawjy: husband.

PEOPLE

Anwar: full of light.

Anya: a woman with large eyes. This is not a typical Arabic name, but when I came across I liked it so much I had to go with it. Like the saying about your eyes being hungrier than your stomach, Anya has the ambition to personally take on every issue she sees- sometimes it's too much for her.

Appollodorus: advisor to Queen Cleopatra, and the one who, as legend goes, helped smuggle her out of the castle, rolled up in a rug, and delivered her to Caesar. Nur, the smuggler, with a rug shop, is a nod to one of my favorite heroines.

Huzzaq: An uncommon Arabic name, meaning clever. That cleverness also clouds his judgment. Huzzaq is in many ways, Ibrahim's foil, just as Noor/Khayal is to Nur and vice versa.

Ibrahim: the Arabic version of Abraham- a prophet and "father of many". I didn't choose Ibrahim; he inserted himself and then demanded I rewrite portions of the story to suit him. Jiddo Ibrahim speaks in riddles and proverbs and has a bit of "the sight". He is not in fact clairvoyant, but has indefatigable conviction in doing the right thing, with extreme patience that it will turn out as it should, in God's own time. In the story, he has no biological children, but he is most certainly a father and grandfather.

Iras and Charmion- Cleopatra's trusted maidservants and confidants. They prayed to Hathor, goddess of love, life and death, and Wadjet, the Cobra goddess.

Jaddah: Arabic for grandmother.

Jiddo: Arabic for grandfather.

Kadir: powerful.

Khayal: darkness or in the shadows.

Mohammed: praise-worthy, the name of the Prophet of Islam. Though the spelling and a quite a few other things about the name are controversial, I chose to use it and the spelling first known to me, because Mohammed, in this story, often brings news or explanation. He is a change agent, a seeker. To paraphrase Rilke, it's the questioning that's more important than the answers.

Nejem: a star, in keeping with the moon and light themes.

Noor/Nur: female and male versions of the same name, meaning light.

Yasmin: a jasmine flower. Yasmin is courageous and willful; singularly and beautifully alive, and a lover of all beautiful living things. Those lucky enough to live inside the sphere of her fierce love call her Yasi, like the one I knew long ago.

FOODS

Babaganouj: roasted eggplant blended into a smooth dip.

Ftayer: Triangle shaped pastry dough with spinach and cheese, similar to the Greek *Spanikopita*.

Fuul: Fava beans pureed with lemon juice and olive oil, served warm, cold or room temperature.

Girshalleh: an Arabic biscotti.

Halal: Foods that are permissible to eat, or a way of preparing foods so that they are clean, similar to the Jewish concept of "kosher". Pork is not halal and not eaten in predominately Muslim countries, thus Khayal misses pork-fried rice.

Halloumi: a type of firm white cheese, similar in texture to mozzarella but with a higher salt content making it grill-able. Other times, salty cheeses are soaked in warm water to reduce the saltiness before serving.

Hummus: a chickpea spread made with olive oil and tahini. The Palestinian version uses less sesame paste and more lemon juice than the Lebanese version most common in the US.

Jibneh: semi-hard white cheese, similar to feta but less salty. Originally made with goat or sheep's milk, it is more commonly made from cow's milk today.

Kaak: a type of bread shaped into a ring and dotted with black nigella or unhulled sesame seeds.

Khubiz arabi: a flatbread, common at most meals.

Lebneh: A sour cream-like yogurt, eaten with many Middle Eastern meals, especially delicious with the Palestinian *mujadarah* (rice and lentils with caramelized onions).

Maftoul: is a dish like couscous, prepared with chicken and chickpeas, and lots of turmeric.

Ma'mool: short-bread pastry filled with dates and nuts.

Musakhan: a traditional harvest dish of chicken roasted with onions, allspice, sumac, saffron, and served on top of taboon bread with pine nuts.

Nabali, Souri, Rasie: three cultivars of olives grown in Jordan.

Sabanekh: spinach.

Shaneeneh: a salted, curdled yogurt drink, and a definite "acquired taste".

Taboon: bread like the Indian Naan or Lebanese Pita, but usually without the pocket.

Tabbouleh: refreshing cold salad of parsley, cucumber, tomato and cracked wheat dish.

Zataar: a spice mixture, largely of thyme, oregano, sumac and sesame, mixed with olive oil and served on bread, as a snack or appetizer.

MEDICAL

GSW: Gun Shot Wound.

Israeli Bandage: to my knowledge, it's never referred to as anything other than an "Israeli bandage" so to remove the "Israeli" would remove the meaning. It is a combat-use blood-staunching tension bandage.

Mid-clavicular line: the middle of the clavicle. Noor finds the middle of Nur's left collarbone, and goes several inches down and in between his ribs. His GSW is approximately in the same location so she has to do the thoracostomy a little lower, after his fourth rib.

Succinylcholine: anesthesia, and one of three drugs used in lethal injection. Succinylcholine injection causes complete paralysis of muscles, including the lungs.

Thoracostomy: small incision in the lung, for drainage. A tube, catheter or cannula must be placed in the incision to keep it open (or it will seal itself back up).

Toradol: a non-steroidal anti-inflammatory painkiller for moderate to severe pain. Though it's not an opioid, I figured that after everything Noor had been through and being awake for well over 24 hours, I could let her pass out after the Toradol injection.

TACTICAL & WEAPONS

Colt 1911 .45: A make and model of handgun and cartridge that have been around in one form or another since the 1870s. This would have been a fairly standard issue model in the 1960s when Jiddo/Ibrahim first joined the military.

Fatal Funnel: Loosely defined as the area within portals, tunnels or other spaces where a person is a completely open target (i.e. there is no cover from attack). Military and paramilitary forces use certain techniques to minimize the size of the fatal funnel, as well as time spent in it. It's an interesting topic, and why you see Ibrahim and Noor moving along the walls, "slicing the pie" and "clearing" rooms.

Flash Bang: stun grenades, designed to explode with deafening sound and blinding light, to temporarily disorient.

Heckler & Koch 9mm: there was quite a bit of debate among my comrades about the type of weapons I should use in the book. I chose the Heckler and Koch 9mm pistol, as common service weapon. As a member of NATO, Jordanian troops are also issued this model, so it fit.

MOLLE: Modular Lightweight Load-carrying Equipment. Think of it as a "go-bag", with the minimal amount of equipment needed in a specific situation.

MP5/MP7: Again, I rattled a few of my military friends with the choice of an MP5 submachine gun, which doesn't have near the same "stopping power" of an MP7. I chose the MP5 is because it takes the same ammunition as the 9mm, saving carry room and reloading time.

PLACES

Amman: the liberal capital city, with a fast-growing modern economy, is also one of the oldest continually occupied cities in the world, with approximately the same population as Los Angeles. When I lived in Amman, there were few street signs and most people gave directions based on proximity to the closest of the eight enormous traffic circles that run east to west through the city. Our home was a beautiful one story limestone cube, with arched doorways, marble floors and a flat roof, from the top of which, you could see the lights on Aqaba on a clear night. In the plot of land in front of and behind our house (which was rented to us- nice digs for an enlisted soldier!) were fields of stones, where Bedouin would often camp for days or weeks at a time. The coexisting contrasts never left me.

Aqaba: 6,000-year-old port city on the Gulf of Aqaba, famously depicted in Lawrence of Arabia film. A beautiful seaside town, with ruins of the ancient city Ayla, beaches, scuba and diving.

Bethabara: near Jericho, and along the banks of the Jordan River. Bethabara is reputed to be the site where John baptized Jesus. Far from a religious stance, I've simply used the site at the end of the novel as indication of absolution and new beginnings.

Dead Sea: the lowest point on earth at almost 1500 feet below sea level, this hypersaline lake is 35% salt and renders bathers incredibly (like zero-gravity) buoyant. Careful shaving before you go- a cut stings like hell.

Hammamat Ma'in: natural thermal springs and waterfalls. An oasis.

Al Karak: the Crusade-era castle an hour and a half south of Amman along the King's Highway. The castle sits high atop a plateau with a view of the Dead Sea.

Madaba: small town in the northwest corner of Jordan, situated in the middle of sites of Muslim, Jewish and Christian religious importance, and home of gorgeous Byzantine mosaics.

Mt. Nebo: the summit upon which a fourth century CE monastery remains with mosaics. Moses is said to have first glimpsed the Holy Land and was buried on the mount. At the highest point of the promontory sits a distinctive serpentine cross (caduceus).

Petra: ancient rock-carved Nabateaen city dating back to 300 BCE. A UNESCO World Heritage Site, and famously depicted in Indiana Jones. Unfortunately, if watch that movie, you'll be disappointed as I was that you can't actually go very far into the ancient Treasury. It's probably the most famous archaeological or historical site in Jordan, and is well worth the heat, tourists and exhaustion.

Wadi Rum: largest wadi, or valley, in Jordan, carved into the sandstone and granite rock formations, and ancient home to many peoples, including Thamudic petroglyphs and Nabateaen rock paintings and temples. Wadi Rum means "the valley of the moon" and is still home to hundreds of Bedouin people.

OTHER TIDBITS

Djinn: genie. There is some variation on this spelling and meaning in many languages and cultures.

Intel: the abbreviation for Intelligence (capitalized).

Jument: a beast of burden, be it ox, elephant, camel, donkey, horse.

Mellon: "friend", in JRR Tolkien's beloved Lord of the Rings series, and the accompanying Silmarillion (Elvish) language he created. Here's where I show my true nerdiness: Gandalf is able to open the sealed gates of Moria by solving a riddle, with an overly simplistic answer, but it's a beautiful passage and imagery. It means all you have to do is say you are my friend and I will believe you and allow you in. For people who live in subterfuge, this allegory of trust is a powerful concept. It's the "password" but it's also the secret to opening your heart and starting anew.

Thamudic: a pre-Islamic, North-African dialect (and people). There are Thamudic glyphs in Petra and across the Sinai region. It's debated, but essentially it's a proto- or pre-Arabic language (somewhat like Latin is to French).

Acknowledgements

Everything that's ever happened to, for, around or before me, had a part in shaping this book. But acknowledgements are like wedding plans that quickly get out of hand, so consider this brief account a courthouse wedding.

In all the vastness of space, we've now been neighbors twice- in Jordan and half a world away in North Carolina. Beyond the many coincidences, Luma Abu Ayyash (the mastermind of Raphanous.com) kindly leant her expertise to the Arabic translations. Any mistakes that remain are entirely my own.

Thank you to Klint Janulis for his expert medic advice and for ensuring there would be no trite ("it's only a scratch") flesh wounds. He, along with Patrick, Dominic and Rachel gave me a crash course on weapons and tactical considerations. Thanks to my brother and my dad for the suggestions and NATO knowledge that got me started; my mom for the medical review, and Sam for lending a poet's ear to *Wadi Rum*. Sincerest thanks to my editors and first champions at 1st Ride- Matt, Lauren, Melinda and Beth.

I am grateful to all my friends from Jordan for the uncommon friendship that rooted this story in me; especially to Yasmin, for unwittingly lending her name.

And to John, who wields his own kind of magic and paints my dreams.

Cover design by John Orrand. Background image adapted from Paul Socker's Untitled picture of Petra at night, taken on June 17, 2009. Posted on Flickr, https://www.flickr.com/photos/paalia/ 3667616539, used under the Creative Commons terms of use. https://creativecommons.org/licenses/by/2.0/legalcode

Amalgamist
Books

About the Author

Cristel Orrand is the author of two published cross-genre novels, *The Amalgamist* and *Khayal*, as well as poetry, nonfiction and short stories. She's currently working on a series of biographies and Southern historical fiction. With an archivist's passion for preservation and detail, she tells the stories of the voiceless and of the past.

Photo Credit Mike Boykin

Cristel grew up in a military family, moving back and forth across the US, and living in such exotic locations as Turkey, Jordan, France and Fort Riley, Kansas. She blends her love of history, people and place in such a way that the settings are often their own characters in her work.

She's a mom, a consultant, a bibliophile, a writer, an historian, a cook, a critic, a gardener, a storyteller, a cancer survivor, a caretaker, a scavenger, and a pugilist, of a sort.

Cristel lives in Raleigh, NC, with her artist husband, pixie power twins and rescue pups.

About the Editor

Lauren Lowther, formerly a web designer, is currently a stay at home mom. She resides in Florida with her husband, children, and two dogs, Ribs and Paddy. Lauren's interests range from history, politics, and religion to fitness and sports.